# WHEN IT COMES DOWN TO IT

LATARSHA TERRY

**ISBN:** 978-1-955148-26-9 (pbk)

A2Z Books Publishing Lithonia, GA 30058

www.A2ZBookspublishing.net

Manufactured in the United States of America.

A2Z Books Publishing has allowed this work to remain exactly as the author intended, verbatim.

# Acknowledgements

I would like to thank everyone who encouraged and supported me. I will be eternally grateful for the words of encouragement, the boldness of the truth when I didn't want it and the love and prayers that I needed. Your smile, kindness and reassurance means more to me than you'll ever know.

LaTarsha

## Quote:

*Most people look in the mirror only to see what the world sees. Challenge yourself to look beyond the mirage of the reflection and truly look at the soul standing before you. Peel away everything the world expects you to be. Stand in the nakedness of truth and be authentically you.*

As she opens the door and sees his face, a feeling of panic consumes her. Her thunderstruck appearance speaks for itself. She tried to hide it, but it's too late. In the second that seemed to last for eternity; she mustered a frightened smile and asked, "why are you here?" Without speaking, he forced his way through the door and all that was left were screams...

Time after time, I am the one who gives advice. I am what you would call a monogamy Queen. The person dead set against anything that would defile the sacredness of marriage. The one who despised those who cheat and lie in a relationship! So why am I caught in this triangle? Why am I the one who's risking it all and putting everything on the line? Where is my help and advice? I can't turn to anyone; that would only make me out to be the hypocrite that I despise. The one who is not worthy of being called a friend, the one who tends to take all the mirrors down to prevent having to look at myself and take inventory of what I have become. Why does something that I know is wrong, feel so right? Am I the statistic that I never thought I would be? Time after time I tried to walk away, but he always finds a way to make me come back for more.

# 1

## *Dee*

Everyone thinks I've got it together. I guess you can say I had a storybook life. I had the life that most dream of. I went to the best of schools, traveled, and had my shit together by the time I finished college. My parents were well-off, but they didn't live as such. They taught me to work for everything I have. I pretty much grew up with the white picket fence with parents who adored their precious girl. I'm an only child so I kept to myself. My circle of associates was small. Who am I kidding? I only have two friends.

One, my girl Porsche. We have been friends since childhood. Porsche was energetic, spontaneous, and adventurous. In high school, she kept the guy's attention. She was a redbone with wavy hair and the body of a 27-year-old at 15. She knew she was cute and fine, and she didn't mind flaunting it. People always saw us together and labeled me as the "quiet one." I was a bit thinner than Porsche, but the shape was there. Hmph, I was what you would call a late bloomer with potential.

Porsche and I were thick as thieves. If a dude tried to holla at me and didn't come correct; Porsche was on their ass like white on rice. She knew I was a bit shy, so she always felt like she needed to protect me. When we hit 12th grade; my potential began to show and I mean something fierce. It was like I woke up one morning and the BLT (booty, legs, and thighs) said "Bitch we here!" With my smooth chocolate skin and curves, my confidence shot through the roof and so did the barrage of dudes trying to get some play. As flattered as I was, I wasn't going, and Porsche remained my protector blocking thirsty niggahs and jealous bitches' asses.

Weeks before graduation, I had been meeting with my advisors and getting all kinds of letters from potential colleges. When I received the letter that I got a full scholarship to Rutgers University,

B-A-B-YYY, that was it! My parents were proud and excited. I always wanted to be an attorney, so this was one of the best schools to get a law degree. The excitement, however, was bitter-sweet and short-lived when I thought about having to leave my best friend.

Porsche came from a family of nurses, so she always thought she would be a Registered Nurse. Her life was pretty much mapped out for her. She said she would remain in Dallas, close to her family and work in Trauma after she became a nurse. We vowed to stay close and on the day of graduation, we partied like there was no tomorrow.

I moved away right after graduation, but Porsche and I never lost touch. We rarely saw one another, but we talked a lot. Most of the time we talked about college and later our careers. She always talked about her Sexcapades, failed relationships and the many men she met. My girl wasn't a hoe by a longshot, but she was what you would call a free spirit. She loved the idea of being in love. She would call and talk about a marvelous man she met. Six months later, as soon as things seem to get serious; she gets bored and moves on. Deep down I thought she had a fear of commitment, but who am I to say anything. I always listened and when asked, gave my two cents, but I never judged. But Shit, sometimes I think I should have been a counselor with all the free advice I gave.

College life was pretty uneventful for me because I had a goal in mind. I graduated a year early and landed a great job at a law firm in Trenton, NJ. I was an up-and-coming Estate Planning attorney. I enjoyed my job, but it just didn't feel like home. I made a rather good salary and things were going well career-wise. I worked with a bunch of stiffs who loved to meet for Martinis and brag about the affairs with their secretaries while their wives were off spending their fortunes. I was the youngest black female in the firm and, I wasn't one of their favorites. They played nice, and they knew not to cross me.

One day out of the blue, a headhunter reached out to me about a job back home and I jumped at the opportunity. I couldn't wait to tell Porche I was moving home. It had been several years since I had been to Dallas and a lot had changed, but there was some comfort in knowing I would be near Porsche.

After I accepted the job, things moved pretty fast. I was set up in a nice apartment that had a beautiful view of the city. Funny, as soon as I got back, we picked up where we left off acting like girls in high school laughing and enjoying girl time, but our conversations were a bit more mature. It took me about a month to get things moved and settled. I left all my furniture and larger items in New Jersey. I donated mostly all my furniture and home accessories and sold a few of the more expensive items. I was starting over, and I didn't mind; it gave me a reason to shop!

Porsche and I started hanging out as soon as I got settled. She would talk about all the parties and jumping parts of the city. She knew I wasn't a party girl, so she didn't dare ask me to go to all parties she attended. She had her own set of friends and a life before I moved back so I didn't expect her to drop everything to hang out with me. She knew the type of person I was, so it didn't bother me if she didn't invite me to gatherings.

Porsche would always tease me and say I'm an uppity daddy's girl because I rarely dated. Honestly, most of the time when the guy found out I was not having sex before marriage, he would weasel his way out of the relationship, but it didn't bother me. It helps separate the men from the boys. I always thought *if I couldn't see a future with the person in five years, then I can't give them what I can't get back in a lifetime.* Hell, I can't say virginity was easy, but I was determined. And it wasn't because I didn't have opportunities. Shit, I was a dime piece with a great body, mind and career and I knew it. And all of my curves were natural. I'm not knocking anyone who wants to enhance what they have, but I was blessed with a 38-24-42 frame that wouldn't quit. I exercised on the regular to keep it tight so if a man couldn't wait for this, he wasn't worth my time. That was my philosophy, but like I said before, not my girl Porsche's. She was cute and still had the banging body and she was definitely in tune with her sexuality. So much so, she often didn't wait for a guy to make a move. If he was moving too slowly for her, she was out. Maybe that's why she ended up in so many failed relationships, but I didn't dare tell her that.

2

About a year after I relocated, I met my other friend, my soulmate, Marcus. If there was such a thing as having a Prince Charming, then I hit the jackpot. As a matter of fact, Marcus was my everything. Nothing and no one could separate us. Initially, I was apprehensive, and I kept him a secret because I didn't want this to be a failed relationship. I was used to succeeding in everything and that included being driven to have a successful relationship. When we first met, I felt he was the one. I never felt like this about ANYONE! He was so patient and kind. He was a lot older, which was another reason why I didn't reveal our relationship too fast.

Marcus in no way looked his age and he wasn't about playing games. He was 6'5' with chocolate skin and had muscles for days. He wasn't too cut like some steroid-pumped bodybuilder, but he definitely would make you do a triple take.

He had the deepest, calmest voice I've ever heard. His voice could be used on one of those meditation apps; hell, I was hypnotized when he first spoke. Unlike men I dated in the past; he never tried to come on too strong. We truly dated. We met for breakfast, lunch, dinner; whatever fit our schedules. He never tried to come over to my house and force exclusivity too soon.

The best thing of all (so I thought) was he didn't pressure me about sex. I figured I would let him know early I wasn't having sex until marriage because if he was not in it for the long haul; I knew this would be his chance to run. He told me he fell in love with my mind and intellect, and everything else would come after I was his wife. After that I was hooked! I was ready to give him every inch of me. He loved to pamper me and loved to travel. We often took impulsive trips and I loved how adventurous he was.

One weekend he surprised me with tickets to Hawaii. After we arrived and settled in; we decided to go to the beach. I wanted to go for a swim, but he talked me into wearing this beautiful beach dress he had gotten me before we left. I got dressed and when I stepped out of the room, he was standing there with the most gorgeous ring I had ever seen! We were married on Kauai Island and it was beyond romantic. It was just us and an ordained minister. Although I was extremely happy and surprised; I would have loved for my parents and best friend to be there. We stayed in a beach house and laid on the sand to watch the sun go down every evening. He catered to my every need and the night we finally made love? Oh my, it was like he knew exactly what to do, when to do it and for how long. I could have stayed there forever. I used to hear women talk about their first times, but I didn't think sex could be any better than this, or so I thought.

# 3

I could barely contain myself on the way home. I couldn't wait to tell Porsche the news! She is going to be so surprised. As soon as we got home, Marcus carried the bags in, and I threw my purse and shoes across the floor. Marcus said he was going to jump in the shower and check messages. He turned to kiss me, and I gave him the quickest peck on the lips as I dashed across the bed to grab my phone and call my girl.

"Hey girl!"

Porsche sounding apprehensive… "Hey girl? Where the hell have you been and why do you sound so damn giddy? Let me guess, Mr. Wonderful bought you another car or took you shopping."

I was cheesing so hard from ear to ear that my cheeks hurt. "Nope! He didn't buy me a car or take me shopping, but you CAN call me Mrs. Dee Alexander now."

Porsche screamed on the phone in disbelief. "Bitch! I know you lying!!!"

I began to scream on the phone like a kid who got their favorite toy on Christmas Day.

"No, I'm not lying ma'am! And I didn't even have to give it up first. And you told me saving myself wouldn't pay off."

"Bitch please, that old ass man? He probably going to give you worms." We both bust out laughing. "Seriously, Dee. I'm happy if you're happy. I can't say I'm not shocked, but you've always made good decisions so y'all will be aight. We're going to have to celebrate. I guess you'll make time for your friend now or do you have to get permission from Fred Sanford, I mean Marcus. Hell, I don't have many married friends so what can y'all do? All the broads I know of who are married are miserable or too afraid to budge without their dude."

"Well, I hate to bust your bubble, but Marcus is the exception and not the norm."

I heard Porsche mumble something under her breath. She always has to have a comeback for everything, but she won't rain on my parade today.

"Well dear friend. Like I said, I'm happy for you. You let me know when you're free and we'll celebrate."

"I sure will. Ooh wait, let me give you a call back with a date. I need to give Marcus a call to make sure he hasn't planned anything."

"See, it's starting already. Okay girl. Catch you later."

We hung up the phone and part of me felt Porsche was a bit jealous of my news, but I quickly shook that thought. Perhaps she was just in a state of shock. I mean I did just spring it on her. Wow, Dee Hampton-Alexander. That sure has a nice ring to it. I feel like the queen of the ball. I felt nothing could destroy my world. Boy, was I wrong.

4

Marcus and I decided we would live at my apartment since it was really close to everything! He had a very nice place, and I must say it was well kept being a bachelor pad. About a week after we were back home and settled we went to his apartment to pack. One thing I didn't like and what he wasn't going to bring with him was this room of black and gold animal print decor. The walls were black with gold print. Just looking at the room made me want to belt out Jazmine Sullivan's song *Lions, Tigers and Bears*! He had it fixed up alright I guess, but I couldn't see that as being a part of my décor.

Between packing and the endless flirting, we weren't getting far. As I put items in a box, Marcus would slap my ass or hold me around my waist. We would smile at each other, then the kissing would ensue. Soon after, we ended up making love. After about the third round of sex, it was clear we would be hiring someone to pack and move for us!

The first three months of our marriage; we had sex every day a few times a day. It didn't matter the time of day. Morning, afternoon, evening; it didn't matter. He was always attentive and made sure I got mine. Around the fourth month of marriage, the sex slowed, and I expected it, so it wasn't a huge shock. He was still as romantic as ever and I couldn't complain. The only thing I could say negative if I had to was his technique which had become a little mechanical; almost rehearsed. I knew like clockwork after foreplay; he would go for the missionary position. All I had to do was swivel my hips a little and he was going to erupt like a volcano.

To tell the truth; I looked forward to the foreplay because the actual fucking wasn't when I got mine anyway. There was definitely no spontaneity in that area. I mean, don't get me wrong; he's good and I honestly had nothing else to compare it to, but when I listened to Porsche and the spontaneity and freakiness she talks about; I can't help but wonder if I was missing something. Nonetheless, that's a minor detail and one I'm willing to deal with as long as he continues to treat me like he does now. I mean everyone can't have everything all the time. I'm sure there's something about me, he wished was better, I guess.

# 5

Porsche and I decided to meet Wednesday at Table 13 on Belt Line Rd. It was in a neutral place to both of our jobs. They have the best Beef Wellington. I was already sitting when I saw Porsche walk through the door. I couldn't miss her. She had on a fitted Royal blue Peplum Pencil dress with some peep-toe snakeskin print heels. She always wore the cutest clothes. I waved for her as she walked in. She saw me and I think we both smiled like we were Nettie and Celie on the Color Purple seeing one another for the first time in decades! I was already prepared because I knew she was going to have some kind of wild tea to spill from the drama-filled weekend she had. How does she end up in so much shit? Sometimes I think that chick lies just to get attention, but that's my girl.

As Porsche walked closer to the table she yelled; "Was sup Girl?"

I was sooooo excited that I wanted to jump up and scream, but I had to keep it cute. "Nothing Porsche. What's new on the soap opera of Porsche Davis?" I know you got some tea to spill.

Before Porsche could say anything, the waiter interrupted with a request to take our drink order. Porsche looked at the waiter and rolled her eyes as she turned back to me. "Girl you ain't going to believe what happened Friday night!!!"

I saw the waiter's frustration, so I turned and asked for a couple of waters with lemon & told him we would need a few moments before ordering. As the waiter walked away Porsche said, "Can you believe that people are so fucking rude? His ass saw me talking. Hell, he could have waited."

"Porsche, now you know had he walked by and didn't acknowledge us, you would be ready to cut up." I love my girl, but she's always had that short ass fuse. It's like she wishes for trouble. Porsche laughed and said, "yeah, you're right. And you know I would be asking for the manager and our food would be free!" We both laughed because we both knew she played that game all too well. There were many expensive dinners we got for free because SHE was unsatisfied with the service or lack thereof.

Porsche picked up where she left off. "Like I said, you ain't going to believe what happened Friday night!"

"What Chick? What happened this time? You always got some shit going on. I'm beginning to wonder if it's you."

Noticing my sarcasm, Porsche looked at me with frustration. I didn't care; she can be crazy with everyone else, but she ain't going to try that shit with me.

Porsche started to blow hard like she was trying to stay calm. "You know what Dee, if you weren't my girl, I'd…"

"You'd what?"

"I'd cuss your prissy ass out, that's what! Anyways, I was at my spot, you know club 64?"

"You mean 69?"

"Hell, no hoe, let me finish telling you. As I was saying, I was at my spot and Davarious walked up asking me to dance.

"Davarious! He's the one that…"

Porsche just looked at me rolling her eyes. I know she wanted to get her story out, and I know my interrupting aggravates the hell out of her, but I needed a laugh for the day.

"As I was saying, Davarious asked me to dance and of course I accepted. You know I wasn't going to let all that pass me by. Well as we were on the floor, Steve's crazy ass came in."

I got nervous for Porsche! Steve is crazy as hell!!! There isn't even a word that can describe him. Once that fool came to Porsche's job and threw a brick through her car window. Had the nerve to attached a note saying that he'll never let go. Hell, they only went out a couple of times and if she's telling the truth, he didn't get anywhere. She ended up having to file a police report, restraining order and everything. "STEVE?"

Porsche leaned across the table closer to me as if I were hard of hearing. "Yeah girl, crazy Steve!"

"Well, what happened?"

"Ohhh now you want to know. At first, you were cutting a Sista off and shit. Anyway, Steve walked up to us saying that I was his woman, and he doesn't know who Davarious was, but he needed to step."

"Say what??"

"Yeah girl, that fool said I was his woman. But that ain't the half… He stepped up to Davarious and I was like, we need to go because Steve was some fool, I went out with once and ended up filing a restraining order on. He doesn't seem to understand that a restraining order means LEAVE ME THE HELL ALONE! Well, Davarious said he wasn't going to ruin his good time by letting some fool roll up on him like he was a bitch. I told him "Baby this is NOT the time, we need to go!" Then Steve grabbed my arm and told me I was coming with him. The next thing I know Steve was getting up off the floor!!!! Girl, Davarious knocked the shit out of him!"

"Girl Nooo!"

"Yes, the hell he did! Steve got up looking crazy talking about I wasn't worth it anyway. Isn't that a trip? My man showed him. If I knew that's all it took, I would have gotten a couple of boys around the block to take care of him a long time ago."

I sat there looking at Porsche with a confused look as she smiled like she was the Freshman girl who went to prom with the most popular high school senior. "What? Wait a minute, your man?"

Porsche's smile faded as she sat back in her chair. "Oh Dee, now here you go. Don't come lecturing me. Tye and I mutually decided not to be together anymore."

"Yeah, but this just happened Porsche. You don't need to jump into another relationship! You're not even over Tye yet. At least that's what you said the other day. Didn't YOU say you know it's best, but you really miss him, and you were going to take it slow."

"YES, I did. You ain't got to remind me of nothing. I know what I said. Shit, I said it! Girl you gotta understand; this is DAVARIOUS! Did you hear me? You've seen him before."

Yes, I've seen him before and boy I understand where she's coming from. The man is fine. If only I wasn't married, I would have dated him myself. He's a clean-cut brother. No kids, decent job, and has respect for women. That's rare these days. It almost makes me scared of him. It seems like a front. Well, maybe this will calm Porsche down a bit. He doesn't really seem like her type, but if she likes it, I love it. She usually goes for the thug-like men. He doesn't look like he will play any of her games. "Well, if he makes you happy then do what you do, but just be careful. Don't get caught up too quick."

"Don't get caught up too quick? What happened to the long-drawn-out speech that I usually get about settling down with the right type of person? Getting someone with husband potential?"

Dee looked genuinely surprised. "Am I that bad? Look Porsche, you're my girl and I want you to be happy, what's wrong with that?"

Porsche giving Dee the side eye started laughing…

"Nothing, if you're anyone but Dee Alexander! You know you ain't ever left anything at that without justifying some long-drawn-out reasoning for it. Even when we were kids, we couldn't even peek while playing hide-n-go-seek, because you thought it was against the rules."

"Let's just say, I'm starting to have a new outlook on things."

Should I dare tell her about my situation? Can I trust her to keep this to herself? Nah, I can't spill this tea; I know Porsche and she wouldn't wait to rub it in…

# 6

It all started on a Monday where I was sitting at the bar outside the firm just to have a drink after this long, dull meeting of the minds. He sat beside me; and at first, I didn't pay any attention, but then he smiled, and it was over…

"Hello, I'm Jay. I don't believe we've met."

I sat there for a moment. I couldn't believe someone still used that old cliché. Besides, I was tired, and I didn't feel like listening to anyone run game. I'm a happily married woman and I didn't have time to mess up what I got.

"No, we haven't met, but my name is happily married."

He laughed and boy when he smiled, the room lit up. I was terribly flattered, but I had to play it cool.

"Okay happily married. Is that your given name or are you just used to being cold and sarcastic?"

Cold and sarcastic? Who is he calling cold? You know I have the mind to tell him something, but I was sort of intrigued, so I continued to play his game of name chasing.

"Why no sir, that isn't my given name. It's Mrs. Dee Hampton-ALEXANDER!"

"Okay, I get it, you're married. I only asked because I never meet a stranger. I think everyone is interesting and I'm certain, you have a lot to say to keep my attention."

Oh my, was the room spinning or what? What are all these emotions I'm feeling? I'm not supposed to feel this way about someone else. I had to keep repeating to myself ("You're married. Dee, you're a married girl, so get it together").

"What makes you think I have something interesting to say?"

"Oh, I spotted you coming to the bar, and I said she is someone I would like to call a friend."

"Friend huh?"

Well, I want to call him more than that. Just look at him. Tall, dark, navy blue Brioni Suit and the shoes; Oh, my goodness, the shoes are on point! Clean and looks like he wears about a size fifteen! Yep, I could get in some trouble with that.

Hmph, who am I kidding? I'm not trying to disrupt the peace I have at home. Besides, he's probably got a woman or three! No man that fine is EVER single or drama-free. Anyway, I'm definitely not touching that entree, but a girl can look at the menu.

"How do you know I'm not some psychotic person?"

Jay sat there for a moment and leaned back as if he were studying every inch of my body. The look and vibe he was giving made me feel like I was a gift he had unwrapped for all to see.

"Well, if you would let me get to know you better, I can judge for myself. But you're not giving me a fighting chance. You're blowing me off like I'm some brother who's shown you the ultimate disrespect."

It was something about his confidence that was a real turn-on. Not only was I intrigued and wanted to hear more; my Cougaritis was jumping around like she was ready to come out and play. I tried to appear nonchalant and uninterested. I waved my hand as if I were giving him the permission to plead his case. "Okay then, Jay."

"Oh, she listens…"

"Yes, I do. I didn't catch your last name."

"It's Jay Smooth."

We both laughed at the absurdity of "Smooth" being his last name. He continued to laugh as he started to move closer to me. My smile faded as I felt it getting a little warm in the room.

"No seriously, it's Jay Crawford."

"Crawford."

"Yes, I know it sounds good. Just think, Dee Crawford."

"That's nice, but the name is Dee Alexander. You're certainly presumptuous."

"I know, but I'm usually not wrong about these things."

"Oh, and you are conceited too!"

Oh, now I feel like a total idiot, presumptuous and conceited, there's no difference. This man is making me sound like an idiot. I bet he calls me on it.

"Naw, I'm just sure of myself. What's wrong with that?"

Whew, he didn't say anything, but I know he caught that. I was so embarrassed. Why do I care what he thinks? Hell he's a total stranger and I'll probably never see him again.

"Well, there's nothing wrong with that. It's quite refreshing to see someone sure of himself. At least you seem to know what you want."

"Yes, I do, but do you?"

As he smiled at me, I began to lose myself in his smile, and my concentration was broken. Marcus walked towards the bar. Startled, I reached out as if I was reaching for dear life.

"Hi Marcus! Honey, I didn't know you would be able to get away to see me."

I sat there almost trembling in fear, but why, I hadn't done anything. I was just being cordial. There's nothing wrong with that. Besides, Marcus is a businessman himself; he understands.

"Hey Dee baby! I see you've met Jay."

Shit! So much for not seeing him again. "Huh, oh yea, yes. Mr. Crawford invited himself to have a drink."

Lord, why does my husband have to know this man? Now I know it's back to reality for me. Marcus looked at me with a gleam in his eyes, he grabbed me around the waist and pulled me closer to him. He turned to Jay and said, "Hey Jay, this one is taken, and I believe I've got the last good one."

"No doubt, no doubt. I'm certain I'll find Ms. Right one day. Well, I've got to get back upstairs. I'll get up with you later Marc. Mrs. Alexander, it was nice meeting you."

Dee's voice almost trembled as she cleared her throat; "Llllike-wise Mr. Crawford."

Jay noticed how nervous Dee was. He tapped the counter with a devilish grin. "Bartender, put their drinks on my tab." He walked away so smoothly as if he were gliding across the floor towards the elevators.

Marcus looked at me as Jay walked away.

"Now that's one of the few brothers who has got his head straight. He's one of the new executives at the agency. He graduated from Brown University and have degrees in cyber security and advertising. I think he's going to be a great asset to the team; especially since there has been talks about expanding."

"Brown University huh? Wow, he must be smart. What brings him to Dallas from Rhode Island? Does he have family?"

Marcus noticing Dee had become a bit too inquisitive. "Hey now, don't go thinking about another man. I'm YOUR knight in shining armor."

Dee slides close enough to feel the warmth of Marcus' breath. She gazed into his eyes for seconds that seemed like an eternity. All the impure and curious thoughts about Jay seemed to dissipate at that moment as she remembered her beloved husband. "That you are honey, that you are."

# 7

About two weeks had gone by and I began to see less and less of Porsche. She was all caught up with Davarious and they seemed to be getting along well. Porsche even decided that she was going to try to straighten up and fly right. She said Davarious was just the person she needed, and he came along right on time. Although I was glad that she's finally found happiness; I can't lie that I'm not a bit jealous. The only time I hear from her is when she wants to tell me about her rendezvous with Davarious. How sweet and nice he is, how she finally realized what I meant about having a good man. That's all good, but I still miss my girl.

*Marcus walked into the kitchen to get his briefcase from the counter. Dee looked disappointed as she noticed he was dressed more for the office and less for the weekend.*

"Where are you going, it's Saturday. You know we had planned to..."

"I know, I know, but we've got this big merger we've been working on, and I've got to get a head start. You don't want people to think your man is a slacker, do you?"

"Well, no, of course not, but..."

"But what? I tell you what, save all that love for me and I promise I will have a special surprise for you when I return. You can trust me. Have I failed you yet?"

"No, you could never fail me. You be careful and remember, when you get home, it's you and me."

"Okay babe. I've really gotta go. See you later."

As disappointed as I was, I tried to appear supportive. I know the company is expanding and I know it would require more time and dedication to accomplish his goal. I looked around the room intensely in hopes to find something to do. Now what am I going to do? Sitting around this house all day is definitely not the answer.

I walked down the hall to grab my robe from the door. Before I could put it on, the doorbell rang... Marcus must have forgotten his key again. I figured I would surprise him at the door and give him something to think about at the office and a reason to rush back home. I threw the robe across the chair and ran to open the door. That's one other negative thing I can say about my hubby. When it comes to losing and forgetting keys, he's a pro! We've had to get the locks changed a couple of times because he misplaced his keys. Well, if that's the worst thing I can think or say about him; I'm sitting on easy street. "Okay sweetie, I'm coming."

Before I swung open our large French doors, I did one last check to make sure my breast were perky, and Marcus' shirt was sitting just right across my ass just to tease him a little. I pulled the door open and lo and behold; Jay's ass was standing there! I peeked around him to make sure this was not a joke.

"Wha, what are you doing here? And how do you know where I, I mean we live?"

Jay with a devious look, "whoa, whoa, whoa. Calm down baby girl. Marcus and I must review the contracts for the merger. He gave me the address and asked me to meet him here."

"Well, Marcus already left for the office so you should be following him."

"Actually, he must have forgotten because I told him I would pick him up. Now that I see you, I see why he changed his mind about me coming here. I wouldn't want anyone to see what you've got going on either."

As I stood there, I realized I only have on one of Marcus' wife beaters with no bra, and a thong. I was just too sure it was Marcus at the door. Dammit! (I guess keys aren't the only things he forgets). All I could say is "Excuse Me?"

"Well do you always come to the door half-dressed? Don't get me wrong, I'm enjoying the view. Shiittt, I knew you were fine, but DAMN!"

All I could think to do was slam the door as fast as possible. I slammed it so fast, but not hard enough to close so it popped back open. As I reached to put on my robe, Jay welcomed himself in.

"Now why did you have to go and do something like that?"

"Look, is there something I can help you with? I told you Marcus is already gone so I think it's best that you leave."

"Oh, I'll leave, but not until I get what I came for."

As he stepped closer to me; my knees begin to buckle. I don't know if it was because I was nervous or if I was consumed with anticipation. Hell, who am I kidding; I was scared as Fuck, but a part of me wanted him so badly. What if Marcus comes home? There is no way I could possibly explain this. I've got to get this man to leave, although part of me desperately wanted him to stay. I continued to back away. I was so fucking nervous, I forgot the layout of my own damn apartment and almost slipped on the step going into the kitchen. He caught me and then forced his tongue down my throat. At first, I thought to fight him off, but I decided against fighting because I was filled with so much desire, not to mention soaked beyond measure. Marcus wouldn't have ever taken me this way! He threw my leg above his head and began to taste me like I was the best dish on the menu. I screamed out as my legs began to shake and my love began to explode like an erupting volcano. And just as fast as it happened; it was over. I immediately felt sick to my stomach thinking of what I had done. I've never been unfaithful to Marcus and never dreamed it would happen in our own home! I pushed against him, and he quickly lifted me, laid me down and walked toward the door. All I could muster up the nerve to say was "Get Out." As he opened the door, he had the most devious grin and said there's more where that came from, just let me know when you are ready."

Before I could think of responding; he was gone. A feeling of panic came over me as I ran to the bedroom to shower. I showered for what seemed like hours trying to scrub away the guilt and disappointment I felt. How can I ever face Marcus? I need to get dressed and get myself together. I've never thought I would betray my husband's trust. To taint my vows to love, honor, cherish and respect until death do us part... Hell, if Marcus finds out; death will come faster than I think. I know this will never happen again. It can't happen again.

# 8

I decided to go for a spin in the new 718 Cayman GTS to hopefully drive away the dirtiness I felt after the encounter with Jay. As bad as I felt, I couldn't help but think about how he took me in a way I had never been handled. How scared I was, but how deep down I craved more. I know, a day at the spa will make me forget and it will all go away. I've been going to the (Sweet Hiatus Spa) for awhile. I called to let them know I was coming. Since I was a regular they would shuffle around appointments just to fit me in if need be. My girl Rosena had been my masseuse since day one and they knew not to even try to book me with anyone else. My girl knows a Sista's pressure points. Rosena was waiting for me when I walked through the door.

By the time I left, I was well relaxed. I went ahead and confirmed my standing appointment. As I hit the e-way, thoughts of Jay started to creep in. Marcus was the only man I've ever been with, and the way Jay made me feel in a matter of seconds, Marcus didn't do in the time we had been married. If he made me feel like that with just his tongue, I can only imagine if we… Fuck! Dammit, I need to shake this shit off and focus. It took me what seems like a lifetime to find Marcus and I'm not going to ruin it with some smooth-talking playboy.

Later that evening, Marc arrived home tired, but presumably glad to be home. And just as he'd promised, he was ready to give me all his attention. I felt just awful for what had happened earlier that day. How could I have gotten so caught up and totally forgot about my man? Just look at him, so gullible and honest. He would run through open flames if it would make me happy and what did I do? I violated our vows in our own home. That's really fucked up. It will not happen again, and I will make sure of that.

Marcus put down his briefcase and as usual; grabbed me around my waist and gave me a kiss on the forehead.

"So, Dee baby, what did you do to stay occupied while waiting on your man to come home?"

Oh, if he only knew, he would be crushed. I'm too afraid to even think of what he would do to me. Well, I know it's not happening again and I'm going to be the best wife I can be because I do not want to lose my husband to one stupid mistake.

"Well honey, I tried to stay busy. I went for a drive, went to the spa, and did a little shopping. But more importantly; I spent most of the day daydreaming about spending time with you."

"That's always a plus. I see you managed to whip up one of your famous dinners. What are we having?"

"I'm having steak and salad and you're having me."

"Oh; I guess I'll be having my two favorite things; steak and my absolute favorite; Dee-lite!"

"Well, since both are ready, which do you plan to have first?"

He slowly grabbed my hand and patiently led me to the couch. Marcus is always so patient and takes his time and I love that, but I couldn't stop thinking about how Jay took me earlier and how fast he made my love come down. Oh, I'm getting hotter just thinking about Jay.

Marcus kissed me and slowly started to undress me as if he were trying to savor every second. He took his time and caressed every curve and inch of my body. Marcus could make me feel like there was no one else in the world but me and I was the queen of it all. Just as I was about to reach the point, we were both waiting for, I screamed with satisfaction. Marcus looked at me with surprise and pleasure and asked where that part of me came from. I immediately thought I was about to give myself away.

Slightly embarrassed; "Honey, I've just wanted you so badly this morning I guess I got beside myself."

Marcus has always known me to be a quiet lover, whispering with excitement, but after the morning with Jay, a side of me I thought didn't exist had revealed itself.

# 9

Porsche called early Sunday morning. I planned to sleep in and daydream about the morning with Jay as well as my night with my beloved. Whenever Porsche called, it was always too damn early, but I couldn't get mad, I was happy to hear from her.

"What's up girl, long time no hear from? What's new?"

"Porsche, girl you know I sleep late on Sundays, and you called to say what's new?"

Porsche laughing…

"Same ole Dee, still complaining; girl you know you're glad to hear from me. I'm the only one who adds some spice to your dull, comfortable life!"

Huh, if she only knew my drama, she would not be laughing, but she ain't ready. Plus, the best-kept secret is the one you don't tell, so I'll be keeping this one to myself.

"Whatever girl. What have you been up to this time? Let me guess, you've grown tired of that fine ass Davarious."

"Hell to the no trick! That man ain't going nowhere. In fact, we are…"

"You are what?"

"Can I finish? Deezammm! As I was saying, we are getting married next year."

A sudden silence was on the phone. I couldn't speak. Not because I was unhappy or jealous, but I just couldn't believe it! Porsche Davis is marrying someone. I must be dreaming…

"Uhhh, gurrrrl congratulations, how, when? Girl, you know you gotta give me all the details. Ooooh, I've got to plan your bachelorette party. Oh, how many bridesmaids you having? I hope you ain't going to have that trifling ass friend Tammy in the wedding…"

"Bitch, slow yo role! I said next year, not tomorrow. Besides, who said I was going to ask you to be at my damn wedding anyway? And lastly, Tammy ain't trifling and deep down, I think she tries to be a good person, but you bet not let that bitch near a man or it's over. (Both Porche and Dee laughed) On the real, Tammy's cool, but you know she has yet to meet a boyfriend of mine in person. She's only seen a couple of pics of Tye and me from a cruise a few years ago. She ain't seen Davarious yet and I'll probably keep it that way."

Dee focused on the wedding… "Girl please, you know ain't nobody else going to help your picky ass with your wedding. And you know damn well Tammy is trifling, sleeping with her mom's husband. And how y'all so-called friends and you never let her meet anyone you've ever dated? Is she going to be at your wedding?"

"Yeah, that was kind of whorish. (Both laughing) I wish I could have seen her mom's crazy-ass chasing her and that man down the street with that knife. I know that was a trip. I haven't decided who I'm going to have at the wedding. Tammy is one of those females you talk to every once in a while and kick it with if you want to get a girls' trip popping'. Other than that, she ain't one I'd ask to be in my wedding."

"Okay, Ms. Davis, soon to be… uuuhhh; what's Davarious' last name again?"

"Winston, get it right trick."

"You know that man must really love you to deal with that mouth of yours."

"Whatcha saying Dee, sumptin wrong with the way I talk. As a matter of fact, he likes it when I talk dirty to him…"

"Girl, you know what I meant, you didn't have to go there!"

"Speaking of going there, what's up with that handsome husband of yours? You haven't mentioned your knight in shining armor yet. Don't tell me there's trouble in paradise?"

"You wish, Marcus and I couldn't be happier. You know how we roll. That man loves me from the top of my head to the sole of my feet."

Marcus walked up behind me and grabbed me from behind. "Oh, he does, does he?"

"Oh honey, I didn't see you there! This is just Porsche on the phone." (Putting Porsche on speaker phone) Porsche chimes in…

"Just Porsche? What are you saying Dee, you know I'm the queen P in this bitch!"

"Porsche is that really called for?" Marcus heard Porsche and laughed…

"Dee chill out and leave Porsche alone. That's my girl. She's always known what she wanted and hadn't been afraid to express exactly how she feels."

"Ohhh hone, that reminds me; Porsche has gotten what she wanted because she's getting married. Isn't that great?!"

"Yes, it is. Who's the lucky fool, I mean man?" *Dee and Porsche both laughed.*

"Watch it Marcus, you know I ain't never been scared of a mutha."

"Oooh, you ladies are too much for me. Sweetheart, I have to step out for a while, but I invited Jay to dinner this evening. I hope that's okay."

"Well, I only planned a dinner for two, but I guess I could…"

Marcus cuts her off, "Oh, that's alright, we're going out tonight and I invited him to tag along. I believe he said he was bringing someone so he wouldn't feel like a third wheel. I told him my baby wouldn't treat him like an outcast, she knows how to make someone feel welcomed. Well babe; I'm running late, I'll be back, and we'll be ready to leave around 7:30 okay? Love you!"

As Marcus left the room, Dee turned off speaker phone and unknowingly took a deep breath as if she was gasping for air.

Porsche said, "Who is this Jay dude and why didn't he invite me and my fiancé?" Fiancé: doesn't that sound good?"

Dee sat in silence as if she heard nothing Porsche said.

"Dee, Dee, damn girl; you act like you in a trance. What's the deal?"

"Porsche, I gotta call you back."

"What? Wait a minute."

"Yeah girl, let me call you later. I'll tell you how the night went. Goodbye."

Porsche sat down holding the phone with a smirk on her face. She knew something was not right. "My girl ain't never act like that before. I ain't gonna press, but I know sumptin up. I'll just wait and see" (laughing as she puts down the phone).

"Why oh why does he have to be friends with this man? I don't know how I'm supposed to act like nothing happened and who is the fake broad he's bringing to dinner? I gotta pull out my best because there is no way some other female is going to show me up. Wa, wait a minute! What am I doing? Jay is not my man, and I should care less about who he brings to dinner. Hell, I'm happy for him. I have my wonderful husband and I don't know him from Adam. It was just a mistake. It only happened once and will never happen again.

As time inches closer, I became more nervous about seeing Jay again. I felt horrible, but I can't help but wonder why I can't get what happened off my mind. As awful as I felt, there was an instant attraction even when we met at the bar. And after the other day... I can't deny it. How can one encounter have me *feenin'* like this? I've never felt this way before. I wonder how he's going to act when he sees me. Let me get myself together; I'm making more out of it than I need to. It was what it was and that's it. But boy, does he know how to work a tongue. If only Marcus could... The phone rang and interrupted my reminiscing.

"Baby are you ready? We're on the way."

"Who's on the way?"

"Dee baby, what's wrong? You know I told you I invited Jay and his date. Are you sure you are okay?"

"Yes sweetheart, I just thought they would meet us there. I didn't know they would be riding with us."

"Actually, we're riding with them. Jay got a limo and we're going to make a night of it. How's that sound?"

"Oh, okay. That's fine. I'll be ready."

As I paced the floor with anticipation, minutes seemed like hours. Finally, Marcus came to the door and asked if I was ready to leave. Jay and his date decided to wait in the limo. As we were getting ready to walk out of the door; Marcus turned to kiss me.

"Baby do you know how much I love you? Everything I do is for you. I would turn the world upside down for you. You are my queen."

"Ohhh sweetheart. Stop it; we have people waiting for us. If you keep this up; we may not make it to the limo or dinner."

"Well let's just call down and tell them we've changed our minds."

"We can't do that; we've got to go. Come on."

As I approached the limo; I tried to get a glimpse of this mystery woman who will be enjoying the same thing I did if the night goes well. Hell, I'm jealous. I kept peeking around Marcus to see if I can see. The windows were too dark; I can't see shit.

As Marcus opened the door; I started to step inside, and lost all my cool points and yelled "oh shit!"

Marcus, startled and obviously embarrassed asked me what's wrong. I could possibly tell him that the trifling heifer with Jay is Tammy. Porsche's whorish friend I talked about but refused to hang around let alone bring around my man. I met her once when I first moved back to Dallas. Porsche invited me to have drinks and she was there talking loud and ghetto. Porsche knew I wasn't feeling her so when I told her I couldn't stay, she understood. I had to think quickly…

"I'm sorry honey. I forgot something. Do you mind if I run back upstairs for a moment?"

Marcus was confused but said, "Of course, sweetness, will you be okay? Jay, do you mind?

"No man, you're good. We've got time."

Marcus dashed behind me…

As quickly as I ran back to our apartment, Marcus came dashing after me as if he was trying to save my life!

"Babe, are you okay? What's the important thing you forgot that could make you to be rude to our company tonight?"

I had to think quickly! "Sweetheart, I do apologize, but I just remembered that it's about that time of the month and I didn't want to be caught off guard. You know that could be really embarrassing."

Marcus looking puzzled…" yes, but I thought you had another week or so before…"

Cutting him off, realizing that he keeps up with my cycle better than I do, "Sweetheart, well you know I stopped taking birth control because we decided we would possibly try to have a…."

Marcus had this childlike innocence in his eyes, smiling at me. "That's right sweetheart, I'm sorry. I can't wait to make you a mother; you are going to be a wonderful mother as you are a wife."

Filled with guilt because first, I haven't stopped taking my pills because I'm just not ready and the fact that my husband is so innocent, so trusting; and what do I do, I almost destroyed what happiness we have and for what? Oh my God! I'm exactly what I despise! I just couldn't bear to tell Marcus that I wasn't ready to be a mom. He was just so happy when HE decided we were ready. I couldn't spoil that for him.

I ran into the bathroom and grabbed a tampon that I knew I wouldn't need, but that was all I could come up with. As I walked out of the bathroom, Marcus grabbed me and kissed me so passionately, with so much love. I wanted to just fall in his arms and cry and confess my soul, but I just couldn't. The pain he couldn't bear. Hell, I couldn't stand to see him hurting. I lightly pushed him away and said, "Sweetie let's go. We've kept your friends waiting long enough."

Marcus stood there looking at me like he was admiring a work of art. "I guess, you're right, better yet, let's tell them we're staying in and work on that baby we want."

Trying to muster up a smile, I grabbed his hand. "No Marcus baby, Let's go. We have plenty of time."

As we arrived outside, Tammy with her trifling ass was standing outside the limo yellin; "Girl, we thought y'all had gotten lost in there! Come on hell, I'm hungry."

Marcus sternly looked at Tammy and turns to Dee.

"Honey, are you going to introduce me to your friend? I assume you know her by the way she's talking."

"I'm sorry, this is Tammy, you know a friend of Porsche's?"

As we walked closer, the gleam from the streetlights showed the jacked-up weave and hoe dress Tammy was wearing. Marcus uneasily smiled as he recalled the stories Dee use to tell him about her.

"Oh, this is the Tammy you were talking about. It's nice to finally meet you."

Tammy wide-eyed and eagerly jumped to grab Marcus' hand. "It's nice to meet you! No wonder why Dee keeps you under wraps, shit you are fine!"

Marcus looked irritated but remained cordial. "Thanks darling, Jay I think we're ready to roll now."

I stepped up and wrapped my arm around Marcus like I was claiming a prize while eyeing the hell out of Tammy. "Sooo, Jay, where are we going since you decided to make a night of this?"

Jay, with a devilish grin, "We're going to this new bar I heard about. I heard the food and music are rather good."

Tammy grabbing Jay's hand, "yeah, that's right, my baby knows how to pick the finest things…"

I thought to myself; Hmph, The FINEST THINGS? MORE LIKE THE MOST WHORISH THING. Tammy was a few years older than me. She had a cute face and the shape of a nutty buddy. She had real broad shoulders and was narrow at the bottom. Her calves looked hard as hell like she had been running for years. There was no smoothness or femininity to her, but she had the confidence of AMERICA'S NEXT TOP

MODEL. Unfortunately, she didn't mind wearing clothes to show every dent, ding, and dimple.

I let out a long sigh while getting into the limousine. This bitch is something else. Eyeing my husband right in my damn face, while grabbing on Jay like he's really her man. I guess he's entitled to one lapse in judgment because he has her on his arm. All I could say in response was, "Huh, I see."

Tammy rolled her eyes and put her hand on what she calls a hip.

"Huh, I see? Biatch, what does that mean?"

Jay smoothly turned to Marcus, trying to avoid the catfight that was about to ensue. "So, man, that presentation is something else huh? I thought the client wasn't going to bend, but you pulled it off. By the time they left, they were more than willing to collaborate with us. Man, I hope to be like you when I grow up."

"Man, you've got all the skills. I wouldn't have you working with me if I felt you didn't."

Boy, does he have the skills! If Marcus only knew how much he wanted to be like him. Not only does he want his job, but he wants his woman too. This distraction he has on his arm tonight is a pitiful decoy though. I decided to ignore Tammy's confrontational comments and sit back and enjoy my husband and be cordial to her and Jay.

It was a beautiful night so the men let the sunroof back so we could enjoy the night air. Tension began to dissipate, and everyone was enjoying the smooth ride, conversation and champaign. Lo and behold, Tammy pulled her hood card and decided to stand up and stick her head out of the sunroof and yell at the cars passing by. I sure hope that atrocity of a wig doesn't blow off her head. Well, then again, maybe it should so she can sit her ass down somewhere. Finally, the limo slows down and turns in. Hallelujah, we're here. Maybe after we go in, I won't feel so paranoid. All night, I've felt like my secret was out on display for the world to see.

Jay stepped out of the limo in his Armani suit, looking phynnne as hell. His chocolate skin was smooth as a baby's bottom and shoes shiny, matching to a tee.

Jay said, "Ladies, shall we?"

I obviously stepped out first because I saw no other lady.

I grabbed his hand and thought I would make a snide remark just to ease my nervousness. "And he's a gentleman too. You are learning from Marcus huh?"

With a sexy smile, Jay said, "I'm learning more than you'll ever know."

Tammy stepped out behind me with her hoochie dress on. "Okay enough with the niceties, let's get a seat and get something to eat. I haven't eaten since I got off."

I don't know why she was lying; she knows she ain't got no damn job! As I observed the scene; I must admit, Jay has taste. It was a genuinely nice place. The music was jumping and from the look of things, everyone seemed to have class. So why did he bring Tammy, a no-class having heifer if I've ever seen one?

I thought it might be a cold night, so I brought a light jacket. Marcus took my jacket from my shoulders. "Babe, I'm going to check our coats and go to the men's room. Will you order me a drink?"

"Sure baby. I'll be counting the seconds…"

Tammy had this apparent look of jealously and the need to outdo me, "Jay, my handsome man, do you mind checking my coat as well? What drink would you like me to order for you?"

Jay aggravated but eyeing me… "Yeah, I'll get your coat, and I'll order when I come back."

Jay returned to the table as the waiter was taking the drink orders. Interrupting me in mid-sentence, "Yeah, could you give me a bottle of Dom Perignon and the ladies will have Armand de Brignac Ace of Spades."

The waiter smiled and said, "Yes sir, coming right up."

It was obvious Tammy didn't have a clue what he just ordered. If it didn't come in a brown paper bag, it was out of her league. A trifling' THOT.

Eagerly wanting to know how he met Tammy. "So, Jay, how did you and Tammy meet?"

"Oh, we kind of just bumped into each other at this club. Club 64, I think. Not my usual type of crowd, but when I saw Tammy, I just couldn't pass up the opportunity to get to know her."

"That's right, you never meet a stranger."

Jay was surprised I remembered our first conversation. "Aw, you remembered, and that's true, I never meet a stranger."

We both smiled as Tammy looked confused and Marcus approached.

"What are you two smiling about?"

"Oh, nothing baby, have a seat. The waiter already has everyone's drink order."

"Why, thank you sweetheart."

"You don't have to thank me; Jay ordered for everyone before I could order for you."

Marcus turning to Jay to shake his hand… "Aww man, you didn't have to do that. My baby always knows what I want…."

Before Jay could respond; Tammy, with her endless need to feel included interrupted…

"Y'all a mess. No one could be that damn happy."

"Don't be jealous sweetheart; I'm sure you'll find happiness like ours one day." (I get nauseous at the thought of anyone making her their side piece not to mention a wife. They would have to be cray cray).

Tammy tuning towards Jay "I'm sure I have, I mean will."

Jay ignoring her statement turned to Marcus.

"Man, the seafood is off the chain."

Marcus was checking out the scene. "Oh yeah? I'm a meat and potatoes man. How are the steaks?"

I caught Jay giving me a slick look… "I feel you; I like a thick steak too. I hear they are really good."

The waiter came to the table and as usual, I ordered Marcus' food. Dinner went okay. We laughed, drank, had small talk and I ignored all of Tammy's irritating comments. The live band began to play. I was bobbing my head to this singer who sounded just like India Arie. Jay and Marcus were eyeing me as if I was the only person in the place. Suddenly Jay said,

"Man, I really like this song. Marcus, do you mind if I cut a rug with your lady for a moment? She seemed to be digging this song."

Jay must have known that Marcus was not a dancing man and Tammy wasn't going to dance if it wasn't something where she was twerkin' her ass to the floor. He knew exactly what he was doing.

Marcus patting his hand on his thigh. "Yeah man, it's cool. Just bring her back in one piece. I'll be watching you."

Jay looking as if he won a trophy replied, "I'll be careful. Mrs. Dee, shall we?"

I didn't want to seem as eager as I felt so I paused as if I was giving it some real thought.

"Well, I guess I can if Marcus insists."

"Oh baby, have fun. Just don't forget who you are coming home with."

We all laughed as Jay, and I headed to the dance floor. Jay took my hand as the smooth sound of the band seemed to flow through my soul. The dance floor was packed. He pulled me straight to the middle of the floor. He made sure I was facing our table as he began to talk. Every now and then he would pull me just close enough so his manhood would graze against me. He was slick enough not to hold me long enough to look suspicious.

"So here we are. I thought I would never get you alone. I can't wait to taste you again. To give you more of what you've been missing."

Trying to appear non-affected by his touch. "My dear, we aren't alone and that was a mistake that will never, ever happen again so just get it out of your head. I love my husband and I will not do anything to jeopardize what we have."

"Seems to me like you already have; isn't lusting after another just as bad as the actual act?"

"What makes you think I'm lusting after anyone?"

"I saw how you've been cutting your eyes at me all night. I could tell you were jealous when you saw me with ole girl. Why do you think I picked her? I know more about you than you think Mrs. Hampton-Alexander. I know more than you know."

Uncomfortable, yet eager to know what he meant, I inquired as to how he knew I would know Tammy. "So just how do you know I knew her?"

"Like I said, I know you better than you think I do. I'm a patient man. I study and always get what I want, and you know I want you."

Slightly afraid of what I was hearing I backed up far enough to look up at him. The look on his face was a look I've never seen on anyone. It was unyielding and devious. As the band switched to another song, I saw this as my opportunity to head back. As we walked to the table, I saw Marcus pretending to care about what Tammy was saying. Funny, I know when he's pretending to be nice and when he's interested in someone's conversation. Tammy turned to see us coming.

"About damn time! I thought I was going to have to come out there and get you. Why are they playing all this jazz and slow R&B shit? Ain't no Rap up in here?"

Sensing Marcus was ready to leave. "I hope you all won't be too terribly disappointed if Marcus and I turn in early. We have an early day tomorrow."

Seeing the relief on Marcus' face. I always know when to bail my baby out. He turned to Jay.

"Yeah man, we've got a big day planned. We got to lay it down early."

"Cool man." Jay waved for the waiter to bring the check.

"Put this on my tab."

Marcus looked surprised yet thankful." No man, I can't let you do that."

"Yes, you can, and you will. You can buy me lunch one day."

I needed to go to the ladies' room. For one I've got to keep up this story of me not knowing when my cycle will be here, another I got to get myself together. Being that close to Jay made me so wet, I thought my juices would flow down my leg at any moment.

"Sweetheart, I'm going to the ladies' room. I'll be right back."

As Jay handed the waiter his credit card. He offered to grab our jackets from the coat check. He knew damn well the coat check was near the ladies' room. A slick mutha…

"Marcus man, could you escort my lady to the limo and as soon as I pay, I'll be ready to get you and your lady home safe and sound."

"Sure man. Make sure no one snatches my baby up, while I'm away."

"Oh, I'll be sure of that. I know you would just be a lost man without her."

"You know it man!"

Marcus and Tammy walked out as I headed to the ladies' room. Suddenly, I was startled as Jay busted into the stall.

"Jay, what are you doing?"

"I'm getting ready to lick those juices before you wipe them away. I know you wanted me out there on the dance floor. You need me to taste you, to hold you and take you."

"Jay, no this isn't right. I love Marcus. This needs to STOP."

Before I could push him away, he pushed his head under my dress and moved my panties aside with his tongue as if he were looking for a pot of gold! His tongue was so thick and warm as he slid it in and out of me slowly and then fast until I was about to explode. I grabbed his head and pulled him to me as if I was trying to drown him with every drop of cum, I had left. He put both my legs on his shoulders and began to suck my clit like he was sucking a thick milkshake.

My legs began to weaken, and I could feel the juices run down my leg as he licked up every drop. He slowly let my legs down. As I stood there shaking helplessly and dazed, I wanted more, and he knew it. As he reached down to unzip his pants, we heard two drunk girls fall into the bathroom laughing. I was so scared; I just knew I would be caught, and this would be the end of me. Thankfully, they left, and he dotted out of the door. Before he did; he smiled and said,

"I thought it would never happen again. You better get cleaned up before Gullible ass thinks his beloved, faithful wife has gotten lost."

"Oh, my goodness, Marcus!"

I hung my head in shame, cleaned myself up as well as I could and headed to the limo. The ride home was as awkward as it was when I walked to the car and saw Jay with Tammy. I tried to make small talk but couldn't stop fantasizing about what had just happened. It seemed like it took hours to arrive home. When we finally reached the private gate, the car barely stopped rolling before I jumped out and said my goodnights. Marcus was a bit more social, but of course, he hadn't just betrayed our vows as I did for the second time. I know I said it before, but this time I'm serious. It won't happen again.

# 10

Bright and early that morning, my phone rang. Before looking I knew it was Porsche. She always calls me too damn early and I knew Tammy's skank ass couldn't wait to tell her she was out with me and my perfect husband as she calls him.

"Hello"

"Girl, we got to stay in contact more often. Hell, you're really missing me and that's why you've started hanging with Tammy. I knew I was your only friend, but damn! I don't even know you anymore."

Porsche was laughing her ass off and she was right to a point; she didn't know me. I didn't even know myself anymore.

Not finding the humor in Porsche's little joke, I said; "What's up girl, I knew she was going to call you. Believe me, it was not planned. You know Tammy is not my cup of tea."

Porsche cut me off; "Enough about Tammy. Who is this man she keeps ranting and raving about? She claimed he puts her in the mind of Tye. Talking about he is all fine and shit. Who is this mystery man?"

"You know what, he does resemble Tye a little, but he's just a bit more built and a little taller than Tye though. But how does she know? She's only seen his pic, right?"

"Girl, I told you Tammy can sniff out a man in 12 feet of snow. Yeah, she only saw a pic of me and him. I guess she figured he was taller by comparing me standing next to him. Hell, I don't know, Tammy's ass can lie too. You know that." Huh, I sure hope my Tye hadn't gotten that desperate. Anyway, I'm sure it wasn't him; he's long gone (mumbling under her breath) and he probably won't be back."

"Your Tye? And I thought that was your girl. I know you aren't calling your girl a THOT. What do you mean he won't be back?"

Porsche sounded aggravated by my questions....

"You know what I meant; I don't want Tye's ass. I've got Davarious. And yeah, she's my girl, but we both know how she is."

Uh-huh, she still ignored my question about him not coming back, but I won't pry. I know there was more to the story than she told me, but I'll leave it alone. I got my own shit to deal with. "Anyway, how is your dream man?"

"He's cool. What's up with the mystery man though? Tammy said she felt like he was watching you most of the night. Shit, she claimed y'all danced and you left Mr. Marvelous Marcus at the table to entertain her."

"See why I don't like that Bitch? She always exaggerates. He works with Marcus at Cole-Lax Advertising, and we danced to one little song. Girl, I was just being nice, I was ready to get home to spend private time with my baby."

I believe Porsche could tell by the tone of my voice that there was more to it than that, but she didn't say anything. Seems to me we've both got secrets, she hasn't been straight up with what happened with her and Tye and I sure as hell am not gonna say what's up with me.

"Yeah girl, I hear you, private time with your boo huh. Well, I'm going to have to meet mister; uh what's his name again?"

"I didn't say."

"Hell, I know you didn't say, but what is it? Damn!"

"His name is Jay, Jay Crawford."

"Why does Crawford sound so familiar? Oh well, it's a common name, I guess. Well girl, I just called to get the dirt. D and I got some plans later today, so I've got some errands to run. Don't stay away too long. And Dee?"

"What"

"Be careful girl."

And as soon as she said that; she hung up. I wonder what she meant by be careful. I know she can't possibly think there is something up with me and that man. I wonder what's the real issue with Tye. It's something up and I'm going to find out. First, she was so in love with him and then she said they decided to go their separate ways and now he's not around at all? I won't worry about it, but something isn't right with that.

# 11

## Porsche

As Porsche hung up the phone, she thought about the years of friendship and how close she and Dee have always been. While she got dressed to run errands, she thought about their conversation. "Dee been my girl for years and I would go to the ends of the earth for her, but some stuff you just can't tell. Some things you just can't tell anybody no matter how close you are to them. I wonder, does she really think that I'm that naive that I don't know she is hiding something?

I don't know if it was more to this Jay dude or if there is trouble in paradise, but I know my girl. She always has to be perfect and have everything in order and she seemed too defensive and too eager to prove she and hubby were still in wedded bliss. She just doesn't know how badly I want to share the truth about what happened with me and Tye. Do I dare tell her the reason I left and the reason why Tye left town? Now is not the time. Maybe never.

Lying in bed with Tye had always been one of my favorite pastimes. I loved the way he was so sensual and attentive to my needs. It was almost like he knew every inch of a woman's body. He knew exactly when, where, and how long to touch me in every area of my body. I couldn't see myself even thinking of being with someone else. I knew he would be the man I would spend the rest of my life with. The only thing that concerned me was Tye could be very isolated at times. He would have these awful dreams that would wake him, and he would be in a cold sweat. I've never seen a person so afraid of a nightmare.

He never cared to discuss what it was, so I just comforted him until he went back to sleep. I prayed that over time my love would help all the bad dreams go away. He was so mild-tempered and understanding. Even when I knew he was mad about something; he would just smile and rub his hands together and tell me it will be okay. When he needed to cool off, he would go for a run. He always seemed to be better when he returned. Who could ask for more? He was my true love. Well, I guess I could ask for more.

See, Tye and I never made love. At least not in the traditional sense. In fact, he never tried to go all the way. His touch and attentiveness were enough to make me explode, and he treated me so well, going all the way seemed a little insignificant. I mean, I knew it would happen someday. Besides, Tye was somewhat old-fashioned. He told me he wanted to wait until I was all his and since he made me so happy; I was good with that.

One day, after one of his long runs he came in and sat beside me on the bed. Out of the blue, he looked at me and said, "Baby, you know I love you right?"

"Yes Tye. I know you do. You look worried, what's wrong?"

"I have something serious to talk to you about. I want you to just listen to me baby. I want you to have an open mind and try to understand where I'm coming from."

"Tye, you are scaring me sweetheart. Is, is it someone else?"

My heart was pounding as if I had run a hundred-meter dash. I just knew Tye couldn't cheat on me, he loved me. We spent every waking minute together. The only time we weren't together was when he went on his daily runs or when he went to the gym. Come to think of it, he's a huge workout fanatic. I bet he's been slipping with some bitch when he claims he's at the gym. I'll kill him!

Tye smiled at me with such a look of love and sincerity, it seemed to calm some of my fears.

"No, no baby. Nothing like that at all. I must tell you something though. I've been holding in for quite some time and if we are going to marry, then I only think it's fair that you know everything, no secrets whatsoever!"

Although I felt some relief, I was even more frightened because honestly, I didn't know much about his past. I guess we always assumed that we both had pasts just as everyone does, but thought it wasn't serious enough to mention. I trusted him and he trusted me. It was never an issue, until now.

"Okay Tyrell, what is it? I'm listening."

"Sweetheart, this isn't easy for me. I, I, well, I've been seeing a doctor for a while now, for a few years, five to be exact.

"Baby are you sick?"

"Please just listen to me. I'm not sick; at least not anymore; I'm not. You may think otherwise after I tell you this. You see, the doctor I've been seeing is a psychiatrist. She's helped me through a lot of unresolved issues I had and helped with, with uh being comfortable with who I am now."

Oh my God, he's screwing this woman and wants to leave me. How can he be sleeping with someone else, and we haven't even done everything? What the fuck? I can't sit here and listen to this shit. I'm going to do some serious damage to his ass if he wants to up and leave me. This can't be happening. My mind started racing and I was so focused on not jumping across the bed and choking his ass, I didn't really comprehend what he said. I've got to calm myself down and play it cool.

"Go on."

Tye looked at me with tears in his eyes as if he was about to burst. I've never seen so much fear in a man in my life!

"Porsche, I use to..."

"You used to what?"

"My name was Tylea. I've been on my own since I was a kid and things happened to me. I was forced to turn tricks."

Is he shitting me? Get real. If this is his ideal of a joke, he has a really messed-up sense of humor. This shit isn't funny. I can't help but laugh, but the laugh quickly faded as I looked into his eyes.

"Whhaa, wait a minute. WHAT THE HELL? WAIT, Tylea? Are you telling me you're a muthafuckin woman? How? When? Hell, you don't look like no fucking bitch. What the FUCK is this about? Look Tyrell or whatever your name is or was, if you want to leave, then leave, but don't give me some bullshit about you being a woman. The way you are with me? I'm a woman, I would know another bitch. WAIT? Is this why you wanted to wait until we're married to make love? Are you telling me you ain't got no damn dick?

I mean, I noticed you shy away from me touching you. Is this why you always shower alone? Why you never stay the entire night? You told me it was important for us to keep something sacred and making love for the first time on our wedding day was all you asked. I believed you dammit! I believed you. You explain yourself right now! We cuddle and I feel that you obviously enjoy lying next to me. What's that? You got the something down there Tye. How the hell do you think I'm supposed to believe this bullshit? This is the most bizarre and absurd shit I've ever heard. Fuck you Tye! Just admit it, you want to leave. You could have come up with something a whole lot different than this bullshit!"

*For some reason, through all my ranting and raving I believed him, whoever the hell he or she is. I could look at him and tell how hurt he was. Although I was pissed as a mutha, I still loved him, and he owes it to me to tell me the whole thing. As I sat there, I realized he had never shown me any childhood pictures of his family. I'm in a DAMN nightmare right now…*

He sat there with a stern look and said, "Look Porsche, do you think this is something a man would make up just to leave? Baby, I love you and you deserve the truth. I was a woman at one time, and I lived a life for the streets. I left home at age thirteen and well, me being 13 years old, I couldn't get a job, so I had to do what I needed to do. I got hooked up with this dude who in the beginning took me in and treated me like his daughter but that didn't last long. I'll never forget one day we were having dinner and he told me that if I wanted to stay with him and he protect me, I had to earn my keep. I didn't know what he meant, but I soon found out. He brought in this dirty nasty man and told me I had to go in the back room with him. He told me I had to do whatever he wanted me to do."

I could see the pain, anger, and fear in Tye's eyes. This was a look that I've never seen before. I was disgusted yet intrigued and wanted to know everything. He continued....

"At first the man made me take my clothes off and told me to lie down on the bed. He proceeded to kiss me and lick my body. I can still smell the stench of his body mixed with sweat and old cologne, and the alcohol in his breath. He took his clothes off and made me...."

I could see the pain as Tye began to sob. I couldn't help but feel sorry for him. I couldn't imagine going through anything like that as a woman, nevertheless a child.

"Baby, you don't have to go any further, I understand..."

"Oh, but I do. My therapist told me that if I ever got the nerve to tell someone else, this would be the point where I was really beginning to heal. I want you to know what you mean to me, and I need you to know the truth. As I was saying, he made me... he forced me to... A child! Can you believe that shit? I didn't even know what a dick was supposed to look like let alone have sex with someone. Sick bastard! And just as soon as it started, it was over. I saw him walk towards the man who took me in and handed him some money. That was the start of my everyday life until I was 17."

"You mean you endured that abuse for 4 years? But how?"

*Porsche seemed to drift off as if she were daydreaming… (This all makes sense now, Tye told me all this stuff about making love not being important, the shyness, and isolation? How he never thought about having children. I wasn't too messed up about it since I never wanted any, especially since…)*

"Porsche! Porsche! Baby, are you listening to me?"

Don't baby me Tylea, Tyrell, whoever you are!

As fast as I said that I felt guilty. Tye looked like a lost animal in the wilderness. Shit! Why the hell am I feeling guilty about expressing my anger? As hard as it was, I know my ranting and cursing would not make this better. I abruptly stopped screaming, took a deep breath, and apologized for yelling.

"I'm sorry, Tye this is a lot to take in."

"I know, now you want to know how my becoming a man came into play?"

"Hell, that ain't all I want to know." Tye ignored my comment as he looked down at the floor with tears in his eyes.

"Well, I was never attracted to men. Even as a child, I just didn't feel normal. Deep down, I knew who I wanted to be.

Growing up in South Boulevard and being around nothing but Pimps, I saw how men seem to have the power, be in charge and got what they wanted. There was no way I wanted to be with a man. Most men I know saw women as weak, as nothing, and as objects. I wanted to love and protect whomever I was with. I wanted to hold someone and love them as I needed someone to love me. Being a woman and going through life in that way was not an option for me. Not only did I despise men for what happened to me, but I also wanted to be one of the few men that treated women with the respect they deserved."

As twisted as that shit sounded, I understood. I didn't agree with the women are weak and nothing shit, but for the sake of argument, I didn't think this was the time to show how strong I was. As hurt, as I was and as much as I loved Tye, I knew in my heart I couldn't be who he needed me to be. I felt like I had been kicked in the chest by someone who showed no mercy. I sat on the side of the bed in disbelief. I was so damn angry, and as much as I wanted to CLAP BACK at him with some real foul shit to try to make him feel what I felt at that moment; I couldn't bring myself to do it. I couldn't be another person to destroy who he wanted to be... who he needed to be. As hurt as I was, at that moment without a second thought, I knew I wouldn't get past this.

Tye raised his head and stared at me like a puppy begging for a treat.

"Porche, please say something. I know it's a lot to take in. I know that. I wanted to tell you from day one, but I knew…"

"YOU KNEW WHAT TYE? You were afraid I wouldn't understand? You thought I would mock you? Well, I guess we will never know because you didn't give me the chance!"

"I know, and I don't expect you to make a decision about us. I know it's a lot to process."

I looked at Tye and couldn't help but laugh, there was nothing funny, but I had nothing left in me to do but laugh.

"Huh! A lot to process. There's nothing to process. THIS, ME, YOU, US can't happen. This whole relationship was built on fucking lies from the start. You can't expect me to come back from this. I'm only glad you told me before tricking me into marrying you."

"Porsche, don't say that!"

Tye, I'm going to ask you one time and one time only. LEAVE!"

Tye's eyes filled with tears as he glared at me in disbelief like I was the one who lied. He stood up and walked towards me as if he wanted to hold me. I can't lie like I didn't want to just fall into his arms and sob, but I refrained. I stood by the door as he slowly opened it and walked away. And just like that, he was gone. That was the end of me and Tye.

# 12

## Marcus

I try my best to be the perfect husband. Go to work, worship my wife, and want to be a family man, an all-around good guy. Well, all of this may be so, but that ain't the half. I've made mistakes in the past and I promised myself that I would be the best husband and spend my life making up for my past. I love Dee. She's caring, honest and loves my dirty drawers. What she doesn't know is that I knew Tammy before seeing her that night with Jay. Tammy started as a H & Q (Hit it and quit it) of mine back in the day. You know, call her to meet me at one of my cribs, hit that pussy and quit it when I'm ready. She soon became one of the best Bottom Bitches I had, and she knew her role. She was trifling as hell, but she knew not to play with me.

Shit, in my time, I had the game on lock. I kept my head low, my soldiers working and my security on point. Yeah, before I knew my wife, I was a lot different. People didn't know me as Marcus, but the infamous King Pin Xander. I did things I don't care to think about or relive.

What my wife doesn't know is that night at the club; I was all too willing to let her dance with my man Jay. That gave me the opportunity to make sure Tammy kept her fucking mouth shut. I know the bitch. Not only is her pussy like seven-11 but her mouth is too. Stay open all the damn time. She talked a lot of shit, but when shit got real, she knew how to play her role. I taught her well. Truth be told seeing Tammy's ass reminded me of old shit that I hated about myself. A BITCH like Tammy can bring out the worst in you. All in all, Tammy agreed to keep the shit copacetic because she knew I had some shit on her that would fuck her life up and neither one of us wanted our skeletons out.

The night we arrived home from the club, Dee and I curled up on the Pearl White Italian sectional sofa she talked me into buying. I must say my lady had impeccable taste and kept the house on point. Had she not been an attorney, she definitely would have been a successful interior decorator.

Dee was laying on top of me as I wrapped my leg around her like I was trying to hold her for dear life. "Sweetheart. Did you enjoy our evening with Jay and Tammy?"

Dee looked up at me as she patted my chest. "Oh, it was okay. I would have rather just spent my time at home with my husband and proved to him just how much I love him."

"Well, why don't you come over here and show daddy just how much you miss him."

"With Pleasure!"

Dee proceeding to kiss me slowly on my chest and moved down to my stomach. She always loved to lick my nipples and around my navel because she knew I would stand at attention like a soldier in the Army. She licked the shaft of my dick like she was trying to savor every moment. She knew just how to deep throat it like she never had a gag reflex in her life. Initially, I had to train her because I was her only, but she was quick to learn. I loved the way she made me feel. She was good at head, but like most women; she didn't give it often. Although she seemed to love it, I learned that she only did it when she wanted something. I wonder what it is this time, a purse, shoes, a trip out of town? What? Oh well, who gives a damn. She knows what to do and I love it.

I'm much older than Dee, but when we met, it was like I struck gold. She was sheltered didn't grow up or know much about the hood, so she didn't know anything about me or my past. By the time she moved back, I had laid a new foundation and had a new life for myself. She was an up-and-coming attorney at a major law firm downtown, and I was an established advertising executive in the same building.

I watched her for weeks before I decided to see what she was about. Every day she would come to the bar for lunch; have a ginger ale spritzer; politely turn down the men who approached her and always carried herself like a lady. Hair was never out of place and spoke so eloquently and intelligently. I mean my baby was approached by all kinds of men. I must admit; a lot of well-put-together; wealthy men of all ages and ethnicities. One thing that got me is she stood her ground and didn't go for the okie doke.

One day I noticed her in one of the black dresses I love to see her wear. It fitted in all the right places. Tight enough to be sexy, but tasteful. She seemed like she had had a long day, so I decided to make my move. I ordered her usual with a note. *"I noticed you seem to be having a long day; I hope this lifts your spirits."* I gave it to the bartender who in turn said "Man, you know you're wasting your time. That chick ain't budging for a brotha. She may be diving." I laughed as I ignored him and said, "I'll take my chances."

I made my way to the elevators and the bartender looked puzzled. He laughed and said, "Smooth; you aren't sticking around for the diss." I told him "Naw; I'm playing my cards right and I bet 21 on all black." As the bartender shrugged his shoulders; he said cool and gave her the drink. If she smiles; I'll make my move. If not, then it's not the time. I saw her tell the bartender she didn't order the drink and he nodded towards me as I pretended not to pay attention. She read the note, smiled as she eyed me up and down. I knew my shit was tight; so, I had no worries in that department. I smoothly got on the elevator and went back to my office.

I made sure she didn't see me for about a week. You know a week is just about the time a woman will give up unless you come across one of those crazy bitches and I was confident she didn't fit that description. One Friday evening she was sitting at her usual spot, and I decided this was the day. As I made my way across the room; a flash from my past came crashing through my mind. I thought about how I treated women, how I stole and killed. All of a sudden, a feeling of desperation and remorse came over me. Then I thought about how much strength it took to re-invent myself and how much I have changed. Shit, the past is the past; if I get this woman, that will be all I need to make amends and show myself I can be the man I was meant to be.

I sat next to her and asked, "Did you enjoy your drink?"

Although she tried to play it cool; she nonchalantly said; "Oh that was you?"

As if she did not know it. I saw her checking me out at the elevator.

"Playing indifferent? Cute."

"Yes, it was me. My name is Marcus Alexander. I hope that small token added some sunshine to what seemed to be a gloomy day. It is nice to officially meet you Mrs…….? I didn't catch your name."

"It's Dee. Dee Hampton. Likewise, Mr. Alexander, but you really didn't have to do that."

"Yes, I did. I always said my future wife would never have a dreary day if I had anything to do with it."

"Your wife huh? And you got all of this from sending me a drink?"

"A man always pays attention and learns what a real woman needs."

Dee rolling her eyes with a devilish smirk... "Confidence, I like. Cockiness, I don't. Which category do you fit Mr. Alexander?"

"Please call me Marcus."

"Okay Marcus and call me Dee."

From there we were inseparable. We met for lunch or dinner, whichever fit our schedules. We seemed to have the same goals and desires in life. What I like most is she kept it casual and when I made a move, she didn't diss me, but she wasn't too eager to oblige either. I liked that. As a matter of fact, we waited almost seven months before anything other than a hug and hand-holding took place. As odd as it was, I didn't mind. She made me feel so good, pressing for sex was the least of my worries. Besides, I've done enough fucking in my past to last me a lifetime.

I had plenty of time. I was ready for wifey material. I've had enough hoes to keep every street corner in Oak Cliff filled and I was done with that shit. When I got out of that last shit, I used all my hoe doe and decided to re-invent myself and build my empire. Dee would be the woman to reap the reward of all my past shit. Man, speaking of old shit; I couldn't help but think about Tammy's bitch ass. She bet not fuck this up or I'll peel that muffin cap back with no problem.

# 13

## Tammy

Shit, the other night was fucked up. Dee just don't know I know her bitch ass husband and he ain't nothing like she thinks he is. Shit, that Busta use to beat my ass until I couldn't see for days. On the stroll for his punk ass night after night. Doing jobs and making drops and all I got out of the deal was a whipped ass and fucked up self-esteem. Well, I bet he didn't know I was a true G, and I was going to come out fine.

I met Marcus's ass when I was a teenager. Mom kicked me out over her boyfriend after I tried to tell her he was making his late-night creeps in my room when she went to work. Do you know 'dis trick didn't even believe me??? Fourteen years old and out on the street because her ass didn't want to be without a man. Ain't that a bitch! Well, I ain't going to lie, it was hard as hell. Trying to find friends' houses to sleep over, begging for food. Too young to get a job, too old to want to go to some fucked up foster family.

Hell, I knew better than that. Get put up until the uncle or daddy feels like playing with some young pussy? Nah, I'll take my chances on the street. At least, I could get put up in the hotel a couple of nights a week and make a few dollars with this kitten. *(Laughing to herself)* Grown-ass men wanting a young girls' kitten vs. a woman. Men are fucked up. That's why I'll never trust one of those muthafuckas.

After a while, the streets became easy for me. I even had my regulars. One of my tricks was an old ass man, and he was into a lot of crazy shit. He paid well, so I did what I had to do. One night he picked me up and I could tell he must have gotten some bad shit because his ass was high as a kite. This sick bitch wanted me to fuck him and his old wrinkle-ass wife. Ain't that some shit? Now I was all about my paper, but a bitch got limits. I ain't munching on no OLD WRINKLED muthfuckin' carpet. Ain't cleaning them muthafucka's either. At least not without getting some real doe. Shiiiitttt, for that bullshit, I had to triple my price.

That piece of crap got so pissed off, he slammed my head into the corner of his car bumper. Bitch had an old ass deuce and a quarter, and you know dem bitches hard as hell. Split my shit wide open. I laid there bleeding and still as hell. I was in so much pain. I couldn't see shit and couldn't even say shit. I guess he and his punk ass wife got scared and thought I was dead. You know, they left me lying right there in the damn parking lot of the motel. I just knew I was going to die right there. I could see it now; the newspaper would read…Here lies a COLD ASS BITCH ON THE COLD ASS GROUND. Ain't that some shit. I laid there coming to terms with meeting my maker. The sad truth is, I didn't even have a clue where I would go, heaven or hell. I figured after the hand I had been dealt in this life, anything was better. As I laid there in pain, suddenly I felt someone lift me up and kept telling me to hold on. When I got to the ER, my head was the size of a basketball. I heard the doctors ask someone if they were my next of kin. I heard a man's voice say I was his cousin. His voice was so deep and soothing, I didn't know if I was dying, and it was the Lord himself coming to get me. Cousin? I ain't got no damn cousin that would come get me, but I felt so safe, I didn't care who it was. I just wanted to make sure that trick was long gone.

I heard the doctors say I would be here for a few weeks with the injuries I had. I was so scared; I still couldn't see SHIT. A Bitch's vision was fucked up. After two weeks, the swelling seemed like it would never go away. As more days came and went, the swelling started to subside, and I could see a glimpse of light. At my side was a knight in shining armor. A man with a silky chocolate skin and a voice that could make a nun's panties wet. I could tell he was much older, but when he introduced himself, I melted.

"Hi, I'm Xander."

"Xander," what kind of shit is that? Xander." What the fuck ever. Okay.

"How are you feeling? I rolled up and saw you lying in the lot. You gave me a scare sweetheart. I didn't think you were alive. Do you know who hurt you?"

"Yeah, I know. I ain't gone stress it. I just know I bet not come cross that bitch or his wife again."

Xander laughed. "Slow your roll baby girl. Seems like they got the ups on you this time. The cops wanted to know if you know the assailant and if you are pressing charges."

I tried to rise, but my head started throbbing, so I laid back on the pillow. "Charges? I ain't pressing no charges, I need to get out of here and make some money. This fucking up my rotation."

Xander gently pushed me back down and covered me with the blanket that had fallen on the floor. "Wait, you don't have anywhere to go? What do you mean by your rotation?"

I wanted to cuss his ass out for acting stupid-like, but I kept my composure. "Look, I 'ppreciate everything you did for me, but I gotta go. I'm losing money."

"Hold on, hold on baby girl. Where are you staying?"

I think dis negro slow, didn't I just say I'm losing money and it's fuckin up my rotation? Any street dude knows that means I'm a bitch out here in these streets making my paper. I got my tricks that I rotate through weekly... tha fuck man. Xander looked at me with this devilish, yet soothing smile... "Girl, let me help you out. You seem like you need help getting on your feet and I have an extra crib or two you can lay in until you get your stacks up."

As much as part of me was screaming no, something's up; I couldn't help but take him up on his offer. Shit, I knew it and he knew it. I was homeless, hungry, and helpless. That was the beginning of Tammy and Xander (AKA Marcus Alexander).

That night at the club, Xander or Marcus, whatever he wanted to be called now damn near pushed Dee's ass up on Jay. Hell, I knew he couldn't leave that pimp shit alone. If it's in a man, it's in 'em. Ain't no amount of money gone rebuild that. Xander not pimping is like me saying I ain't black no mo'. Ain't going to happen.

"What's up Xander?"

"I don't go by that name anymore. It's Marcus to everyone including you bitch."

"Ok, okay Xan… I mean Marcus. I know why you stayed back and letting yo girl dance with my fine ass dude. You ain't gotta worry 'bout me. You know I'm a rider. Always have been, always will be."

"You damn right, I ain't gotta worry about you. Bitch you know what will happen if you ever cross me."

Marcus slid closer to me and grabbed me on the top of my thigh and started to squeeze like there was no tomorrow. He continued to throw threats and smiled at the same time. No one had any idea, how much pain I was in as it felt like he was ripping the muscle straight out of my leg. Boy, did that bring back some bad memories. This evil dude could look like he's whispering sweet nothings in a bitch's ear and all at the same time, he is threatening your damn life. That's the messed-up thing about him, dangerous and smooth at the same damn time. No one would ever know Jekyll & Hyde is as crazy as he is. I had to think quickly because keeping a straight face while he whispered horrible threats in my ear and squeezing my leg was becoming unbearable.

"Okay, Marcus, I hear you. You know I'm not going to say anything. I don't want to fuck you over like I don't want you to mess me up."

"Bitch, I can't mess up nothing and that's what you are, a nonexistent, nothing of a hoe. Remember that shit."

Huh, if I can't mess up anything, then why the hell is he tripping? There's no way I would ever say that to him, so I tried to show a seductive smile and said, "Okay, I got it. Now can you please let my leg go?"

This lowdown dirty dog quickly let my leg go and slammed it so hard into the leg of the table.

"I'll gladly let go."

I was all too ready to go as I watched Dee's gullible country ass stroll back towards the table. Jay was fine as hell, but I hope he doesn't think I didn't notice he was feeling ol' girl. Like I said, I'll never trust a man, they're all the same. They all do one thing… Fuck. Whether it's on you, over you or around you; they gon' fuck. As they walked to our table, Dee's smile quickly faded. I guess she realized how much she was cheesing over another Bitch's man. I knew her ass wasn't as miss goodie-two-shoe as she wants folk to think. I wonder if Porsche knows her friend is an undercover hoe. Hmph, I had to laugh at that myself. *Tammy, girl stop tripping, Dee's prissy ass ain't going to do nothing and nobody, but Marcus' crazy ass.*

Marcus said, "It's getting a little late and we have an early day. Are you all ready to roll?"

Looking at Jay with a smirk… "Man, you've danced with my wife long enough, I gotta take her home."

Jay said, "Oh yes, it's cool. I need to spend a little time with my lady here."

Marcus held in a laugh while thinking to himself. (Lady? The only lady at this table is my wife.) "I heard that. Well, we're going to let y'all have it."

Dee said, "Honey, I need to run to the ladies' room before we leave."

Dee always gotta act so damn prissy and shit. I don't see how she and Porsche are friends. Porsche is so laid back and this bitch acts like she always got a gun cocked up her ass.

Jay looks at his watch and I guess it occurred to him he had work to do. He looked at me and said "baby do you mind if we call it an early night? I promise to make it up to you."

Hell, I didn't mind, I was kind of bored anyway. And being here with Marcus's ass & *little miss my-shit-don't-stank* was cramping my style. Besides, as I looked at my watch, I realized I still had time to hit a late hour spot of mine and have some real fun.

# 14

## Jay

Jay stood in his living room reflecting on the night. He was so filled with anger and rage. "These muthafucka's going to pay for everything they did to me. I'm going to make each one of their lives miserable. Payback is going to be a bitch. Marcus running around like he's king Tut, living lavishly off the pain he caused me. Shit, I know that muthafucka. All his skeletons ain't in the closet. And he ain't the only one who had to rebuild himself. Hell, I was only 15 years old when I had to step up and protect mine. Real shit went down, and we decided since I was younger, and never been in trouble, the folk would take it easy on me.

Man was I wrong. Juvenile, then straight to gen- pop in the FCI five days after my 18th birthday. That was fucked up. I did a solid six years for that shit, and it took another five years to rebuild myself. From getting my ass beaten in juvenile and almost killing a muthafucka for thinking he could try to bitch me; to getting released, stacking paper, and creating what is now a slick-talking, wealthy man with one of the top companies in the state? I didn't do too badly, but all that shit could have been avoided if it weren't for Marcus' punk ass. Let's not forget Tammy. She ain't getting off the hook either. (Jay began to smile as he thought about his plan).

Too bad little Dee is caught in the crossfire and will suffer for what she thinks is a perfect husband's sins. I hate to say it but I'm going to enjoy fucking over her too. I've had to live a miserable, messed up life for years while these muthafucka's lived like none of this shit went down. They just don't know; they've screwed over the wrong one. Finally, I'm ready to fix what was messed up for me and mine."

I knew Tammy's trifling ass wouldn't have a clue who I was. She was so damn thirsty, and all she needed to see was a man who looked like he had paper. I watched Tammy for about two months. This bitch knows she hangs out at some grimy places. There was one spot in Uptown Park she went to on Thursday nights. The club played a mixture of R&B, nothing too hype. It wasn't too bad for my taste because calm was the scene, and the owners wanted to keep it that way. I got in good with one of the owners and hooked him up with some advertising ideas pro bono to help put his spot on the map. His business started to boom and so did my confidence with setting things in motion.

One Thursday I made sure I was sitting a couple of seats down from where she usually drools all over some fool to buy her a drink. While I watched her flirt and hit on all kinds of dudes, I began to be disgusted; yet filled with anticipation as I thought about how I would work my magic.

I asked the bartender what she was having, and he gave me an awkward look. "Man, do you want to go there? She craves and gets all kinds of attention. You don't seem like…"

Before he could finish, I cut him off. Hell, I know what she craves, what all hoes crave. I had to play it smooth. "Yeah man, I'm just getting the lady a drink, nothing more, nothing less. It's all good."

The bartender gave me a strange look and just shrugged his shoulders. "She's having her usual, crown and coke. She keeps it simple. Thursday from 8 pm until about 11 pm give or take depends how many crowns and cokes she gets."

"Okay, send her two for me."

As the bartender delivered both drinks, she began to look at me like I was the last Colossal Prawn on her plate. Sad to see a woman that damn thirsty. But who am I fooling? I wouldn't dare call her a woman. I continued to sit at the bar and pretend to watch the game as if I didn't see her. I hope the hoe don't know anything about football because this game is the furthest thing on my mind. She downed the first drink like she was drinking Alka-Seltzer. This chick is more trifling than I remembered. As she gulped down the second drink, I noticed she grabbed her purse. She sashayed towards me bumping into every chair at the bar until she reached me.

"Thank you for the drinks. You didn't have to do that, but I'm glad you did Mr..."

"Jay is my name. You're Tammy, right?"

Immediately, the hood began to surface. She stood back on one wobbly ass leg asking how the hell did I know her and what did I think two funky drinks were going to get me. My first thought was to slap her ass and let her know, no one wants her stank twisted ass but I had to let cooler heads prevail.

"Sweetheart, the bartender told me your name when I offered to buy you drinks. As I said, I'm Jay, I just wanted to offer a beautiful lady a drink. That's it. I hope you're enjoying your evening?"

For a moment, it seemed as if some human side of her surfaced and her face began to soften. She stood less rigid and spoke softly, yet still under cover ghetto.

"I apologize, but these tricks, I mean men think just cuz they buy a drink or two, that's an invitation to some ass. Can we start over and thanks for the drinks?"

This chick couldn't have tact if someone drilled it in her forehead.

I listened to Tammy go on and on about this life of pretense she's made for herself. All the while, I was amazed she had no clue who I was. I know I was just a kid, but damn. I know I look like my kinfolk, and she was all over that. Then again, this bitch was known for being all over everyone. Plus, back then, she was so full of that 4/20 and Crown, she probably didn't remember her name. It didn't matter, if she thought she could get a dollar, she was on it. As I sat there with more disgust, I had to revert to my plan. I see now, Tammy's ass ain't going to be a problem and from what I know about her jealousy and need for attention, this is going to be easy.

After what seemed like a lifetime of Tammy's ghetto ass conversation; I couldn't manage the niceties anymore. I needed to shut this night down.

"Tammy, I've really enjoyed meeting a nice woman like you. Since I'm new in town, I wondered if you wanted to accompany me to this bar and grill this weekend. It's going to be just a colleague and his wife, and I don't want to be the third wheel so…"

Before I could finish, this THOT jumped on me like I asked her to marry me.

"Sure, I'll go. Don't mind hobnobbing with new people. Never know what kind of connections I'll make. Shucks, as long as I can dance and get my drink on, I'm there."

That's all this hoe thinks about… damn. "Oh, yes. Well, put your number in my phone and I'll give you a call with more details. It's time for me to call it a night."

Before I could give her my phone, she snatched it and start dialing her phone so she could have my number. It's all good though. This isn't the business phone. There's no way in hell, I would have her as a contact that's important to me. I feel nauseated trying to smile at this trick. I tapped the counter to get the bartender's attention. I told him I wanted to close out my tab for the night. He looked confused because he knew I don't pay for anything here since I got in with the owner. There was no way, I wanted her thirsty ass to know that, so I left a stack on the counter and told the bartender to keep the change. When she saw that stack on the counter, she looked like a kid in a candy store. I bid her goodnight and I made sure I headed the opposite direction before she got any ideas that I wanted to spend the night with her.

When I got home, I laid back and fantasized about the life I could have had and all the things I missed. The fantasy soon faded as I started to think about how everything was taken from me in a matter of moments. I didn't have a leg to stand on. I went from relaxed to mad like 40 going North. I laid there staring in space. My fixation was broken as I noticed blood dripping from the side of my mouth. Dammit! I was so fixated on Marcus and Tammy; I didn't realize I was biting down on the side of my tongue. I got up and put some crushed ice in my mouth to numb the pain. I downed a glass of cognac and fell asleep across the bed.

Finally, the evening came where we would be meeting for dinner. I was so amped; I couldn't contain myself. All I could think about was finally paying these mofo's back for all they put us through. All the pain, the suffering, sleepless nights… all will be worth it after this. I picked up Tammy in a stretch limo and told her we would pick up my colleague and his wife. Her little simple-minded ass would be so impressed by the limo; she didn't even bother to question why I never had to ask for her address. All that street smarts and a bitch is as worthless as two left shoes. As I pulled up to the complex, I couldn't help but be impressed she did okay for herself. As quickly as the admiration came, it faded, and I became filled with anger thinking of how she got what she did at the expense of me and mine.

I called Tammy to let her know I was waiting downstairs in the limo. There was no way I was greeting her at the door. I got my damn limits. She doesn't mean shit to me and I'm not going to make her think this is something more than just a casual thing. I don't know why women think just because you greet them at the door, it's a start of a relationship or some shit or maybe it's just the females I run into. Either way, I didn't want her to get any ideas. She came running downstairs in that tight-ass, short dress. This broad doesn't have any class, damn. I figured the least I could do was to step out of the ride and let her in.

"Oooohh, this is nice. And roomy! Damn, there's a minibar in here too?"

I gave her the fakest smile I could muster and told her to help herself.

"I hope you don't mind; we are picking up my colleague and then we will head to dinner."

"Fine by me, as long as I got this bar, I'm straight. We ain't waiting for them before we have a drink are we?"

Ugh, you can take a girl out of the hood, but you can't take the hood out of the girl. That's for damn sure.

"No sweetheart, help yourself."

Before I could finish my sentence, Tammy was gulping down a glass of crown straight. I just looked at her as I prayed for patience and focused on my goal. The ride was uneventful and thankfully, didn't take long to get to the office where Marcus was waiting. I texted Marcus to let him know we were parked in front of the building. As Marcus opened the door and got into the car, Tammy seemed to get a little quiet. I introduced them knowing damn well, they knew one another. Marcus and Tammy, both played it smooth and pretended not to know one another. Marcus called Dee to let her know we were headed her way. As much as I was eager to see this thing through, I was more eager to see Dee. Her unsuspecting ass will pay for all her man's sins. Tammy was trying to keep the hype up, but you could definitely tell there was tension in the air.

I gotta give it to Marcus though; he obviously didn't think shit about Tammy because that's about how much attention he gave her… Shit. As Marcus and I talked about work, Tammy tried to interject here and there. Although the ride to Marcus place was only 15 mins away, it seemed like a lifetime with Tammy trying to force her way into conversations that were way above her intellect. We arrived at Marcus' crib and just as I suspected, the doting husband jumped out to get his wife. As Tammy and I waited in the limo, she began to yap on and on about herself mostly. She finally asked how long I had known Marcus, how did we meet, etc. I told her I just met him when I moved here after I accepted this job. Tammy looked towards the window and said, "Hmph."

I could tell by that, she wanted to say something else, but I'm sure fear and common sense kept her from doing otherwise. As Marcus and Dee walked into the Limo, Tammy said, "Dee? That's who he with? Hmmm, okay then Dee."

"Oh, do you know Mrs. Alexander?"

"Yeah, well kind of. I know of her through a friend of mine. She's my girl's girl, but I don't fuck with her like that. I mean we've never kicked it though."

*This Bitch can't even carry a conversation without showing her lack of intellect and grace.* I thought to myself, yeah, I'm sure she doesn't deal with hoes like you. "Oh yeah, well that's all the better."

Tammy began to mumble under her breath… "I guess so, but if Dee knows like I know…"

I pretended not to hear her as Marcus and Dee approached the limo. As Dee started to get in, she yelled and said she forgot something. I laughed to myself thinking she started to freak out at the thought of riding with the man of her dreams and the man in her dreams. Marcus turned asking us to hold up as he ran behind her. At that moment, Ghetto Queen again…

"Damn, what now? Dee is so damn prissy. She is holding up my party time. She needs to bring her ass on."

I had just about had enough of her hood rat vibes, but before I had time to check her ass, Dee and Marcus walked back to the Limo.

At last, we were on the way. I could see Dee trying her best not to eye me and doing her best not to show her disgust for Tammy. We were having an enjoyable conversation when suddenly, Ghetto-Ann decided she wanted to stick her head through the sunroof and scream as if she was on the damn Titanic. As pissed as I was, I tried to play it off and gently grabbed her around what she thought was a waist and asked her to come in. I guess she wasn't worried about her hair, especially since her ass had those damn lemonade braids or whatever you call them. I hate those things. As she sat down, I noticed a piece of lace had peeled up above her ear. A FUCKIN LEMONADE WIG! Damn, who the fuck? This is too much.

We finally got to the place and our night was about to begin. I noticed Dee was digging the music and I knew Mr. Too Cool was not a dancer, I took my chance. I, like a gentleman, asked if he minds if Dee and I cut a rug. I knew he did not want to come across as the jealous type, so I knew he would say he was cool with it. As Dee and I headed to the floor I made it my point to make sure she was facing her man as I mouthed everything I wanted to do to her.

At one point the floor was crowded but I made sure she couldn't help but feel what she needed against her. His ass is so damn arrogant, he never in a million years would think anyone would make a move on his chick in his presence. That's what kills me with this MoFo. Part of him still thinks he's that NIGGAH that everyone feared. His bitch ass ain't shit now and I know it especially since his goons are no longer playing secret security for his ass.

Dee was so nervous and timid, and I liked it. I pressed even more. I told her I would have her no matter what it took. A brief look of fear came across her face, so I downplayed it and backed off. After the song ended, we headed back to the table. As I turned to walk away, Dee flew past me as if she were being chased by a thief. She was. I was the thief who was going to take her mind, body, and soul. I was going to take everything she thought she had.

As we got to the table, the air seemed a little thick. I was certain Marcus had time to catch up with Tammy. Yeah, make 'em all uncomfortable. Discomfort brings mistakes; mistakes bring confusion and dismay. We had dinner and drank a little. I had to keep my eye on Tammy, I didn't need her ruining the reputation I built for myself any more than my being seen with her already has. Dee seemed rushed and made up some excuse about them having to leave early and would catch a cab. I insisted on ending the night as well and paying for the bill. Marcus didn't want me to do that, but I smoothed it over by telling him to buy lunch one day. That would appease him enough, so he would still look cool and not seem like he's taking handouts. Dudes like that always like to be in control, but what he doesn't realize is I'm playing chess while he is playing with checkers. I've already anticipated his move.

We agreed on the bill as Marcus attempted to walk Dee to the restroom. I already had a play for that as well.

I told Marcus, "Man, the coat check is right near the restrooms. After I grab my credit card, I'll grab our coats and make sure no one snatches your lady if you promise to make sure my girl gets to the car safely."

Marcus was quick to oblige. "Bet."

I was betting on Marcus agreeing to see the skank to the car because he wanted to solidify Tammy's silence. Dee quickly walked towards the restrooms with an awkward worried look on her face.

*(Man, this is easy as fuck. Dis negro, so into trying to impress people, he doesn't realize, I'm finna fuck his life up)*

As I watched Dee head toward the restroom, all kinds of thoughts went through my mind. I could pay someone to rob them, or better yet beat Dee up. That'll hurt old Xander to his core. Yeah, I know what they use to call that Mark Ass in the streets. Hell, Xander had the streets sowed up at one point. Shit, if you mention his name now in some circles, people clinch up like they tryna squeeze a diamond out their ass. Well, I ain't scared of the trick. He ain't what he used to be. More importantly, I'm not who I use to be. I'm not that scared little 15-year-old boy anymore. I'm a grown-ass man. A grown man who is going to fuck up this perfect little existence old' Xander/Marcus has created for himself. I stood near the restroom close enough to see if she was alone. This must be my lucky night! The last little drunk bitch just staggered out of the bathroom with her spandex catsuit-wearing friend. It's now or never…

I walked in as Dee was straightening her clothes. I made sure the door closed behind me. "Don't be too quick to zip up that skirt," (Dee looking surprised).

"Oh, you didn't think you were going to get away from me that easy, do you? I told you on the floor I was feeling you and I know that pussy is wet and feeling me too."

Dee turned around, "Look, my husband is waiting at the car with YOUR DATE! I need to go, and you need to stop this."

As I continued to walk towards her, I pushed my head under her skirt. As much as she wanted to resist me, I could tell she wanted me even more. With an evil grin, I knew I had her. Let the games begin…

# 15

I was lying in bed daydreaming as Marcus walked in and brought breakfast in bed. I thought to myself; My man always knows how to make me feel special. I love him so much. I wish that damn Jay never walked into our lives. I can't help but think about how deep down I wished Marcus was more like Jay when it came to…

Marcus put the tray down on the bed and sat beside me interrupting my thoughts. He grabbed my hand and kissed it and had this serious look on his face.

"Sweetheart."

I sat there a little nervous, but I had to keep up with the hype. "Yes, my beloved."

"We need to talk."

Shit, Marcus never comes in saying we need to talk! I hope that man hasn't told him anything. I'm going to kill him if he fucks up what I got. "What's wrong dear?"

Well, remember when I mentioned the big merger we were working on? Well, as you know, we closed the deal but...

"But what baby?"

"Well, they want someone to be the front man for this advertising deal in Japan, at least for the first nine months and they asked me to spearhead it."

"Japan? Baby that's a lot to take in. I mean that's so far away, and we don't know any damn Japanese!

Marcus smiling..." I know baby and I know you've got your own thing going on here. I was thinking I would pitch Jay to them and see what they think. I mean he's lived in Japan before from what he said and he's very qualified. Plus, he doesn't have a family."

Dee almost smiling thinking she's found a resolution to her problem... "Yes baby, I think that would be a good opportunity for him. By the way, you said he doesn't have a family?"

"Well, I don't believe so. Shit, he never talked about any family. He mentioned his parents died when he was young and said he never really knew them. He said something about an aunt who raised him but never mentioned siblings. He seemed like a bit of a loner if you asked me. The couple of times I asked about family, he shut it down, so I didn't bother to pry. If the man doesn't want to talk, he doesn't want to talk."

Dee thinking out loud…" That's true I suppose."

Marcus noticing Dee staring into space… "Hey, why the concern about this man and his family? What about coming over here and making a family with me?"

Marcus brought up having a family before and I know I said I stopped my pills, but I'm not ready for that. He knows I'm not. I plan to open my own firm and a child would throw a big wrench in our plans. "A family baby, REALLY, but we said…"

Whoa, whoa Dee, slow your roll baby. I know we want to make sure our careers are in place and in no way am I'm rushing this. I have a gut feeling things are going to settle down soon; especially if everything is squared away with this Japan situation. I know things are going extremely well here and I have several big accounts. This Japan deal is the most lucrative and would set us up for a while. In fact, you would be able to quit working if you wanted. The only drawback is we would need to uproot what we have just for a while, and I don't think you want to do that.

Marcus knows damn well I don't want to go to Japan. I mean I have my friend and mother here in the states. I would much rather Jay take his ass and I can forget he ever stepped into our lives.

"Honey, I understand, and you know I support you in everything… But JAPAN REALLY?"

We both laughed and Marcus kissed me so gently before we started to enjoy our breakfast.

# 16

# *Tye*

After Porsche and I broke up; well, she pretty much dumped me, I decided to move to Atlanta. I needed to get away from Dallas. I couldn't bear to be in the same city with Porche, knowing how I felt about her. I couldn't lie though, I still made trips to town every now and then just to make sure she was all right. I know that shit sounds stalkerish, but just because she left me, I couldn't turn off my feelings for her. It just doesn't work that way. I heard she was dating someone and happy and that's all I ever wanted for her.

I can't blame Porsche for ending it though. I should have told her in the beginning, but how does that conversation start? I should have given her more credit. I'm sure she felt betrayed and lied to. All the things I wanted to prevent anyone from experiencing, I did to her. Maybe if she somewhat understood my life; she could have been more open-minded. Hmph, who am I kidding? Hell, if someone did that to me; I probably wouldn't have taken it well either.

I heard Jay was back in Dallas. We haven't talked much, well let me be real; we don't talk. He's so damn angry and I get it, but I can't hold on to the past. As awful and horrific as it was; I had to try to let go. The last time he and I spoke; he was filled with so much rage and talking out the side of his neck; I told him I couldn't be a part of his life if he was going to choose to remain angry all his days. He told me I was a dumb bitch for letting *them* change me. I know he's hurting, and as much as I hoped; he can never understand who I am.

When I was around 21; I was still turning tricks. One day I met a chick when I was leaving one of my usual Johns. It seemed like we clicked immediately. She didn't judge me and understood my life. I mean I had a 9-5 just like everyone else. I turned my tricks at night and during the day I chilled with my girl. As far as I could see, that would be my life and I almost came to terms with it. One day my girl said she could get us hooked up where we wouldn't have to live like this anymore. Shiittt, she sold me the American dream. Make money work for me while we travel the world. My girl mentioned it off and on, but I thought it was all pipe dreams. One day she brought up how she knew I wanted to transition, and she assured me she would always be there regardless. Hell, I never had anyone down for me so that won me over.

It was our 6-month anniversary, so I wanted to do something nice. I was planning a trip to Florida, but my girl insisted on California. She mentioned she knew someone who could put us on and put some real money in our pockets. She said we would be set up and wouldn't have to worry about a thing. She kept selling this pipe dream and telling me I would have enough money for my operation, somewhere to live and more importantly, I would never have to trick anymore. I hated it. I hated men. I hated having to zone out day after day, time after time just to get chump change.

About a week before our trip, my girl asked me to just meet this OG who could put us on. She claimed he was a real dude who took care of business but was not to be fucked with. I decided to meet with the man about this business venture ole girl kept going on about. Dude's name was Xander. Man, this shit was almost an honor. To the average person, Xander was a myth. You would hear stories here and there, but no one ever got close enough to say they knew the man.

This faceless man was well heard of in the hood, but it was rare that you encountered anyone who actually knew him. It almost seemed unreal when my girl mentioned him. And for her to know him well enough to know the myth was real, was unimaginable. If Xander himself wanted to talk to us, I knew it was something big about to go down. This man was so well known and feared. I had no idea this was the OG my girl talked about. Hell, how did she know him? Well, I was in such awe that I was in his presence, I couldn't worry about that.

Man was so smooth, but I heard he took no prisoners. He would get rid of anyone who even looked like they were going to cross him. The main thing is the poe-poes couldn't and wouldn't touch him. He had a legit business, but the streets knew there had to be a side hustle. You just couldn't place him with no ill shit. I mean he didn't have a normal hustler's cover up legit gig. No shit like a barbershop, repair shop or hot wing joint. No obvious shit like that. I heard he owned an upscale Jazz Bar and Grill.

It was a nice prestigious place and no riff raff could get in. For the most part, I heard only attorneys, doctors, real executive types could be up in there. If you didn't have on a suit and pulling six-figure stacks, you couldn't get in. From what I heard there was a membership fee just to be able to walk up in there. I heard you had to go through some interview type of shit and people checked you out for weeks to ensure you were who you said you were. I once heard about this female who found her way in with some high-profile exec. She talked about how there were five levels to that bitch.

The basement entrance was an underground check-in. Someone was checking your membership and passing you through some scanner type of shit like airport security. The first floor was a custom-tailored suit shop. The second floor was Bar and Grill with a live band and the third floor was a Cigar & Hookah Bar. There was one other level, but no one I ever met knew what went on. People spread all kinds of crazy rumors, but no one knew for certain. All I know is ole' girl came back talking 'round the hood and I don't know how true it was, but I heard Xander had her taken care of.

Come to think of it; ain't nobody heard from or seen her ass anymore. They said the dude who brought her in had to pay a hefty fine for bringing in a tactless female. I don't know if the fine was monetary or if he had to pay in another way. One thing about it; Xander didn't go for anything or anyone bringing attention to his establishment. Thing was, Xander lived a low-profile life. No expensive cars or clothes that anyone could see, but we all knew he had weight.

Shitttt, I knew my girl had street credit, but damn. She always seemed cool and always collected, but around this man; she acted like a nervous schoolgirl. I guess I understood, but it did give me an uneasy feeling about all of this. Against my better judgment, I decided to indulge in the conversation. One reason, no one, I mean no one said no to Xander. Especially a wanna-be, struggling, hungry bitch like myself. Xander said my girl mentioned we were going to California and said "we" wouldn't mind dropping off a package at an address on the way to Cali.

I'm not stupid, I knew this was some foul shit, but he made it sound so simple and said it would be worth my while. As an incentive, he gave us $100,000 in cash and said that was just pennies considering what we could have once they confirmed they received the package. Shit, when he handed over the money like he was giving me five dollars; I almost passed out. I ain't never seen that much money in my life! I was cheesing, my girl cheesing and all I thought about was having a better life.

Before we could get the money good, my chick immediately wanted to shop. I had to be the voice of reason. I told her we didn't need to do shit until we got back home and made sure all went well. She reluctantly agreed but understood.

Xander gave simple enough instructions. We couldn't fly, no other riders and drop the package off at the address on Tuesday between 3:45 pm- 4:10 pm. I thought the instructions on the time were strange, and the long ass drive we were going to have to take was a drag, but hey; it was $100,000.

I told Xander we needed to rent a car. He gave specific instructions where we could rent and to only use cash. We agreed to leave Saturday just to make sure we were in Cali early and there would be no hiccups. He looked at us both and just walked away. Two dudes said the package would already be in the rental when we got there. This man thought of everything. Ole girl was like a kid in a candy store. All Friday night, she kept daydreaming and talking about what she was going to do with her share and how we were getting out, blah, blah, blah…

I was up early Saturday morning, ready to do this and move on to my new life. As usual, she was late. She hated getting up early. That's the one thing about my chick. She was always late. I had a knot in my stomach all morning. I kept shitting and couldn't hold any food down. My nerves had me all messed up because I had never done anything like this. My girl kept reassuring me it was a simple job, and my nervousness would pass. As we were putting our luggage into my little hooptie, a car pulled up.

"Aye yo sis, can I roll wit 'chu?" As I looked out it was my young ass brother. We go months without seeing one another. I worry about him, but I can't take care of him. Hell, I can barely take care of myself.

I said, "What did you do? Why you 'round here?"

"Yo sis, I need to roll with 'chu on the real. I can explain later. Can I pleassseeee go with you?"

I looked at my girl and then my brother. He had a look of despair on his face. I know Xander said no extra riders, but this is my kid brother. I can't just leave him. Besides, what can a kid get into? My girl never met Shawn before, but shit, she didn't care. She had money, 4/20, brown liquor and was going out of town; she didn't give a damn who went. I attempted to introduce them, but my brother was trying so hard to jump into the car and dollar signs were in my girl's eyes; neither of them really gave each other a glance. They both said wassup and he jumped in. I wasn't feeling it, but something in my gut told me he needed to get away. He was living with friends from what I last heard so ain't no telling what's happened.

"Man come on. You got clothes?"

"Naw, but I got money, I'll buy something along the way. Can we go now?"

We went ahead, loaded up and rolled to the rental place. I know my damn brother is in some shit. Man I just want this over with so I can start my new life.

We pulled up to the rental and told them we wanted to reserve a car. The receptionist was this nonchalant ass bitch who seemed to be having a difficult day. She asked where we were going. As soon as I said Cali; her whole attitude changed. She said she had my rental waiting and ready to go. It wasn't anything extravagant. A Jeep Cherokee, it wouldn't stand out too much and it had enough room for our bags and the three of us. My girl jumped in the rental before we got the keys good. As she looked around the truck, she said "I don't know, this may not be enough room for the shopping we're going to do." She noticed my look of frustration and turned around.

As my brother was helping load our luggage; he said "yo sis, someone must have left a bag in here." I quickly interrupted him and said, "Yo man, let's go." I figured he got the hint. He got in the truck and didn't say another word. My heart was pounding out of my chest as we pulled off the lot. After we got on the e-way, I could begin to breathe. We drove for hours and hours. I listened to my gal talk and dream while my little brother slept and listened to his iPod. Since I was doing all the driving, I stopped in New Mexico to get a little rest. I got a room for us and made it clear we would be leaving by 9 am on Sunday. After we settled in the room, I decided to have a little talk with my brother. Just as I thought, his ass was dodging trouble. More like an ass whipping. He loved to talk shit with his young ass. He said he was beefing with some lil dudes on the block and needed to lay low. I didn't press or lecture. Shit, I couldn't; not how I live my life. I had no room to say a word. Sunday morning seemed like it came quick as hell. I felt rather good knowing I had my girl and my brother with me and the thought of having a little change in my pocket made me feel a little relaxed. As fast as I felt relaxed, a feeling of panic took over when I realized I was the only one in the room!

I ran to the window and the truck was gone. I called my girl's cell and of course the bitch wasn't on. As I walked back and forth across the room, all kinds of thoughts were going through my head. We're in an unfamiliar state, we don't know a soul. Someone has gotten my girl, my brother and… Oh, shit Xander! What the fuck? Man, if this package is missing out of the truck, it's over. My shit is fucked. As I began to visualize my own funeral, the two of them stroll through the door laughing and high as a fuckin' kite like they had no care in the world.

"Man, where da hell y'all been? You know we needed to be gone two hours ago."

My girl strolled across the room like she had no care in the world; "Babe, will you just chill? Me and lil dude picked up some breakfast snacks and got him some drawers from Walmart. You know his ass left town with just the clothes on his back. Damn, chill."

My damn heart was beating out of my chest. "Chill my ass. We will all be chilling in a fuckin' meat locker if we screw this up for Xander."

My girl immediately seemed to snap back to reality when she heard his name. Man, this man must really be the truth. Sheeeeittt, who am I fooling', I know he is. He ain't to be fucked with.

We got on the road and after another hotel stay and frequent stops; we finally made it to California. I'll need a week to recuperate before we even head home. Tuesday finally came and we rented another hotel not too far from the address. We entered the address in the phone and had it timed perfectly from our location or so I thought. The plan was to get to the address, conveniently leave the package at the side door while UPS makes its stop in the neighborhood. Hence the 3:45 to 4:10 pm timeframe. We left the hotel at 3:20 pm. I checked the traffic and there were no delays. All seemed to be going as planned. We rolled up in the hood around 3:40 pm. My girl was busy eyeing some knock-off purse someone was selling on the corner.

Her eyes were huge, and she was bouncing like a kid in a Toy store. She said, "Babe, let me get this bag really quick, we got time."

I looked at her like she had lost the last bit of sense she had. "Girl you crazy? Nah, we don't have time for that right now. Let's get this done and roll out."

She kept pointing at the purse ignoring everything I just said. She said, "Looks like it's the LAST ONE; it's gonna take me two minutes, look we got plenty of time."

I knew I was messing up when I thought twice about stopping. Shawn gave me a look like don't do it, don't do it. Against my better judgment I pulled over to let her buy the bag. I saw her looking at other shit on the table. A quick minute turned into 25 mins! I yelled out the window and told my girl, let's go now. She strolled to the truck like the world was at her feet. I was pissed and she didn't seem to care since she had that cheap ass bag on her arm. We made a circle in the hood and as we pulled up to the address, I saw the UPS truck like clockwork leaving the neighborhood. I looked at my phone and it was 4:13 pm! My heart sank. I pulled over in front of the address. We briefly debated about who would drop the package. Since my girl was in the front and closest to the house, she jumped out and casually strolled to the door to leave the package. As we got to the end of the street, I put on my right turn signal. Out of nowhere, blue lights were everywhere! Ain't dis a Biatch!

When we get to the station, all I could think about is why my girl felt it was so important to get a muthafuckin purse when all we had to do was make the drop at the designated time and move on. She could have had all the purses in the world.

Of course, when we got there, they wanted to separate us. The first thing they wanted to do was play this good cop, bad cop shit. I'm already hip to this, that game ain't going to work. Besides, they ain't got nothing. Nobody saw us drop anything and we were just here for questioning. Since my brother was a minor, this nice officer let me sit with him until it was time to talk. They took me back and asked who I knew in the neighborhood, what was I doing over there, all the general shit I knew not to answer.

As I sat quietly, they started to threaten me by saying they watched ol girl drop a package of drugs and money at an address. I knew not to say a word besides ain't no way I was rolling on my girl. They questioned us for what seemed hours. Suddenly, the officer left out and came back a few moments later. Dude had this slick grin on his face and told me to get comfortable because my brother and I would be there for a while until they get everything sorted out. He brought my brother back in with me and told us we had one phone call we could make. As we sat there, it dawned on me they made no mention of my girl.

"Excuse me officer? The young lady, um where is she? Where's my friend?"

"Oh, you don't need to worry about her right now. You need to worry about who you and your brother are going to call."

"Sir, why are we being held? What's going on?"

As I sat here confused, I didn't know what to think. Why are they keeping me and my girl apart? Where the fuck is she? "Sir, I don't have anyone else to call. My brother and my girl are all the family I got."

At that time, another officer walked in. She was this big burly bitch with a bad attitude. "Oh, baby girl bailed out. She's gone. I guess y'all left on your own."

"What? Ain't no way in the world."

As I lay in holding in disbelief, I prayed this was a mistake. I mean, I didn't know what I was being charged with, my lil brother wrapped up in this shit and my girl just bailed out and no word. They finally sent in some punk-ass public defender to tell me I'm being charged with trafficking and distribution with the intent to sell. Intent to sell what? I don't even know what was in the damn package. I never looked. I didn't want to know. The public defender said my brother would have to go to detention until our court date. I was in such disbelief, I barely heard anything he said. All I kept thinking about was my girl had to have a plan to help me out. She wouldn't leave me high and dry like this. I attempted to call my girl for days. By Saturday, I made one additional attempt to call her. To my surprise, she answered…

"Yo, what the fuck? Man, what's going on?"

"Look, I told you I didn't want to go with you. I can't believe you; I'll see what I can do to find a lawyer or something. I just can't believe you did this to us."

I was with the phone totally lost because this chick was acting like she had no clue who I was. This was all her idea. She wanted to make this fast money. Now she is acting like she ain't never met me. How could she do this to me, to us? As hurt and angry as I was, she was the only person who could help me. I had no one else in the world. She said she would put some money on my books and try to find an attorney, but I shouldn't keep calling her. As I hung my head, all I could say was "Damn Tammy, why?"

As promised, she would not take any more of my calls. She did however get me a reputable attorney. As he reviewed the extensive list of trumped-up charges, he agreed to represent me and Shawn. He said because I was older, I would do a lot harder time and suggested due to Shawn's age, he would get off with a slap on the wrist. The day of court, the DA and our attorney approached the benched. After a private conversation and a signed statement from my brother; The judge sentenced him to seven years. Part would be served in juvenile until he turned 18. On the other hand, I was given 10 years' probation and a $10,000 fine. Slap on the wrist my ass. This was going to fuck up my brother's life. And where the hell I'm going to get $10,000? Shit, that bitch left with the entire $100k.

A simple ride across state lines messed up my brother's life and mine.

I kept thinking over and over how this girl just ruined my life with no remorse. After my charges and sentence, I was lucky enough to find a distant cousin who said I could live with him. Arrangements were made so I could go back to Texas and I can't wait. I'm going to find that bitch.

My cousin only saw me once after I returned. He had his own thing going and I made it clear I had no plans to stay with him. I knew they wouldn't try to track me like that. Especially since they were able to ruin another young brothers' life. They got their conviction. That's all they cared about.

I asked around the Highland Hills to see if anyone saw Tammy lately. There were a few sightings here and there, but for the most part, she laid low. I needed to get money, so I was back to turning tricks to pay for room and board week to week. One day as I stepped out of the car of one of my tricks, I saw Tammy's ass and she was with Xander! Before I knew it, I yelled *"Yo Tammy, ya Bitch!"* She looked like she saw a ghost. I thought this was my chance to get revenge; instead, Xander drove up and told me to get in. She sat in the front looking straight ahead. You could see her almost physically shaking. Xander pulled on this back street and stopped the car. He said he wanted to commend me for holding my own but expressed his disappointment for messing up a simple task that caused him millions. Immediately, I knew I was in trouble.

I didn't know what to think. Was he going to kill me? And why was Tammy with him after what went down? Why did no one try to help me and my brother? I had so many questions, but I knew damn well I wasn't going to ask Xander a thing.

He pulled off and drove a short distance. The next thing I know, we pulled into an abandoned building. It was dark, wet, and cold. There were maybe two lights working and it was very creepy. We sat there in silence. I was too afraid to speak and Tammy knew not to speak but Xander obviously had a plan. Without turning around Xander began to speak.

"As I said before, I commend you for holding your own while you were down, however you had very simple instructions that you failed to follow, and you put a huge dent in my business."

Before I could think to respond, Tammy started to yell; "But Xander, let us expla…" Before she got out the word "explain," Xander punched her in the face with what seemed like all his might. Her head hit the window and she laid there, slumped down in the seat. I was so afraid; my body was frozen. He didn't even take a second look at Tammy as he turned to me and told me to get out of the car. I was so scared it seemed like it took my legs forever to catch up with my brain to tell me to move. I decided all I could do was plead for my life.

"Xander, please don't kill me. Look, I'll do anything, please. I paid the price, my brother still paying, and he didn't have anything to do with it."

All during my begging, Xander looked calm, yet I could tell he wasn't hearing the shit I was saying. Suddenly, all I heard was, "Take her."

"Take her? Take ME? Oh, please don't."

As fast as he uttered those words, he walked away, got into his vehicle, and drove away as Tammy seemed to lie lifeless against the car window. I turned around and there were two big burly men and one thugged out female walking towards me. I knew this was it. I would never see my brother again and in my head, I began to try to make peace with God. As soon as one of the men grabbed me, he pulled out a huge needle and I felt a pinch in my neck. Immediately I fell limp from fear and despair. The next thing I know I woke up tied up looking at THE GALVESTON BAY!

One of the men and the female were standing over me conversing about their orders to exterminate the pest. The man tied large concrete blocks to my legs and hands. I was so sick with fear, I threw up all over his shoes. He turned and looked at the female and said, "This bitch! I ain't got time for this shit. Come on man, let's do this and get the fuck out of here."

The female squatted down next to me and shook her head in disgust. She was small in stature, but I could tell by her demeanor, she was the soldier running the show out here. She looked up at him and said, "Man, I've got this, go get yourself cleaned up and I'll meet you at the car."

The big man hesitantly said, "But boss said…"

She gave him a look that could kill and he knew she meant business. She said, "Naw, I said go to the damn car. I'VE GOT THIS SHIT!"

The guy shrugged his shoulders and walked away as if he knew not to challenge her. As soon as he was out of sight, she turned back to me. My eyes became so wide, I thought they would pop out of my head. I decided to try to make one last plea for my life, but she cut me off before I could utter one word.

"Look, I don't know what you did, but if Tammy's ass was involved, I know you got the short end of the stick. God or your momma must be watching over you because this is your lucky day."

As I sat there confused, I noticed she was cutting the zip ties and ropes with the concrete blocks from my hands and feet. I wanted to hug her, but I knew better than to move.

"You better leave Texas and never come back. Don't try to contact anyone, especially not your family or Tammy. From now on, you have no one and know nobody, you are invisible. *YOU GOT THAT!*"

I could barely process what I was hearing. Was this a joke? Where will I go? What will I do? I ain't got nobody so fading in the background ain't hard but I don't have a dime to my name. I guess I can think about all that later. She's sparing my life! Suddenly, she looked at me with gentleness in her eyes. "You remind me of my daughter before she was killed over some dumb shit."

She looked like she wanted to confide in me, to pour out her soul. As fast as the gentleness came, it faded.

"Here's ten stacks. Take this and disappear. If you don't or if I hear you had the gall to come back; I'll kill you myself."

She stuffed the money down my shirt and turned to walk away. She turned back to me and kneeled down again. She looked me in the eyes and without remorse said, "I hope you can swim!" and pushed me off the pier and walked away.

# 17

## Dee

It's early Saturday and I don't have anything to do. I hope to keep it that way. No dinners, no surprise visitors, no emergency calls from the firm. Just quiet and relaxation. Well, I want to relax, but I can't get this man off my mind. I sure hope Marcus can talk Jay into taking that job in Japan. I need him out of my life! I can barely look at myself in the mirror. The guilt of what I've done is almost more than I can bear. I'm constantly on pins and needles because Marcus has become so close to this man, and he means us no good. They work together, they go to the gym and hang out together. Before Jay, I was Marcus' life. He went to work and came home.

We always met for lunch or early dinner at the bar near our office if one of us worked late. Now it's Marcus, me, and Jay. I don't like this. I want him gone. I selfishly find myself daydreaming about Jay. It's like he's wormed his way into my life and won't leave. I keep thinking about the night at the bar. Not just what he did, but the things he said to me. It made me so uncomfortable. What did he mean when he said he knows more than I think? What does he think he knows about me? I wanted to confront him, but I don't know how. I'm afraid to see him alone. It's like I lose all common sense when he's around.

As I dropped my head in despair, my thoughts were interrupted by Marcus.

"Babe, what's on the agenda today?"

"Nothing and I would like to keep it that way."

"Oh, I was just thinking, you haven't talked to Porsche in a while. I'm sure you miss her. You've been so supportive, and I know I've been dragging you to dinners, business meetings, and other things. I thought it would be nice to spend time with your girl. I mean, y'all use to talk all the time. I rarely hear you say her name now."

I knew he's up to something. I haven't talked to my girl in a while, but he's never encouraged it either.

I said, "Marcus, what is this about? What are you up to?"

Marcus grabbed me around my waist and started to kiss me as only he can. I almost melt whenever I'm in his arms. But as safe as I felt and as much love as I felt; my mind would always drift and start to feel guilty. I guess I unconsciously pushed against him, and he called me on it.

"Babe, what's wrong?"

"I'm sorry, I've just been so tired lately. Do you know we haven't pressed pause for weeks? We've been going so much; I would really like a day just to lie in your arms and do nothing like we used to."

"I know, it's been a whirlwind lately. You know things are going so well at work and the better it is the busier it is. And since Jay has come on board, I've been able to make the moves I need to make. I promise things will slow down after this Japan deal."

Why did he have to bring up his name? I'm sick of hearing his name. I'm sick of seeing him. I just want my peaceful life back. "I know and you know I support you. Wait a minute… you asked me about calling Porsche. How did we get on work?"

Marcus looked at me with his innocent eyes and said, "Well, I sort of invited Jay to come over this evening to close out some final details and agreed to throw some steaks & potatoes on the grill. Oh, you don't mind honey, it's for our future. Everything I'm busting my butt for is so we can live comfortably and start the family we want eventually. I figured you could invite Porsche over since you two haven't seen one another in a minute."

"Ohhh, I see. That's where all the buttering up comes in. He's NOT bringing Tammy right, Marcus! That's where I put my foot down. I don't want her in our house."

"Of course not. I know how you feel about her, and I don't even think they talk like that. I think that was just a casual thing."

"Well, I'll call Porsche, but this isn't a double date thing. She's with Davarious."

"Honey, of course not. I just didn't want you to feel obligated to entertain. You and Porsche can play catch up and shoot the shit."

I looked at Marcus and laughed, "Shoot the shit huh?"

He walked close enough and slapped me on my butt and gave me a kiss on the cheek.

I said, "That's not the cheek you need to be kissing."

Marcus turned and laugh and said, "Oh I know, in due time. Just wait until everyone leaves tonight. Better yet, let's not wait. Let's give them something to see!" Marcus was so tickled; he could barely finish the sentence.

"Boy, stop it. Fine. I'll call Porsche now."

I dialed Porsche's number and before it rang, she answered.

"Dee, girl you aight? Where have you been? What's been going on with you?"

"Girl, I'm good. I'm glad to know you haven't forgotten me. We've just been so tied up and Marcus dragging me to all these business dinners, etc...."

Porsche let out a sigh of relief. "I thought you had been kidnapped or something. You didn't answer my calls, I didn't know what was going on."

Didn't answer her calls. What was she talking about? I've not gotten any calls from her at all. "Porsche, I think you're losing it. I haven't gotten any calls from you."

"I called your ass twice last Thursday and once yesterday. It went straight to voicemail every time."

Last Thursday? I was at a business dinner with Marcus and my phone didn't ring. I don't know I only left my phone to go to the restroom, but that was it. I didn't see any missed call. I decided not to dispute the issue. Besides, I was extremely happy to hear from my girl. "Girl, I don't know what happened then. What do you have going on this evening?"

"Not much. Davarious and I were going to just chill at the house. Why, what's up?"

"How about you two coming over here for dinner? Marcus is putting steaks on the grill. He and Jay are going to discuss some business stuff and I thought you and I could catch up? I'm making a double portion of baked potatoes and my famous seven-layer salad you like so well."

"Well, Davarious…"

"Oh, bring him too! That would be great!"

"Are you sure Marcus wouldn't mind? I mean you did say he and the guy will be discussing business. Speaking of the guy. Tammy doesn't mention him too much now. She says they talk every now and then, but not much else. I guess they didn't click too well."

*Aggravated at the sound of Tammy's name.* "Humph, does Tammy click with anyone for long? Well, I don't know what's up with them. I don't ask and don't care to know. Wait, here comes Marcus now. Let me tell him about Davarious."

"Marcus, Porsche says hi and Davarious is coming over too. Is that okay? She said he didn't want to intrude if you guys were talking strictly business stuff." Marcus kissed me and replied, "That would be great. I'll put on another steak."

Porsche laughed: "Y'all still nasty I see. Can he wait until you hang up before giving you one of those loud ass smacking kisses? Ugh. Girl, what time do we need to be there?"

Ignoring Porsche's teasing. "Six o'clock and be on time please. You know how you do. I should have said 4:30 pm so you could arrive on time."

"Dee, we'll be there. Oh, won't Jay feel out of place with the four of us?"

"Chile, please. He doesn't seem to ever be bothered by being outnumbered. He always seems cool and collected. See you at 6 pm!"

I tidied up the house and made sure everything was on point. The beverage bar was ready, the potatoes were baking, and the salad was as beautiful as ever. Marcus had the steaks sizzling and the smell was flowing through like heaven. I don't know if I was happier to see Porsche or happy that she would be a distraction and I wouldn't have to worry about Jay's devilish looks piercing my soul. Like clockwork, Jay arrived about 30 minutes early bringing some expensive wine and offering to help. I can't see how Marcus doesn't see the looks he gives me. He's so damn slick with it though.

"So, will it be just us three this evening?" As he moved closer, he whispered "better yet, me and you?"

I tried to ignore the comments and answered loud enough for Marcus to hear, "No my close friend and her fiancé will be joining us. Too bad you didn't bring a date."

Marcus walked in and yelled for him to come on the patio.

"Aw man, I sure hope you ain't burning nothing back there. Let me give your wife this wine and I'll be on my way." He waved and handed me the wine. As I took the bottle, he mumbled "why would I bring a date when I got my woman here?"

I quickly turned and tried to shake off the nervousness I felt. As I began to relax, the doorbell rang, startling me. I rushed to the door, and it was Porsche and Davarious. As I opened the door, Porsche said, "Dang I know it's been a while, but you look like you saw a ghost."

"I'm sorry, y'all come in. How are you Davarious? Has Porsche been driving you crazy?"

Davarious laughed, "Crazy in every way I love."

"Oh goodness, y'all still acting like you're in love; how sweet."

Porsche rolled her eyes, "Whatever Dee. You and Marcus aren't the only two people in love. Now where is Mr. Perfect, I mean Marcus?"

I turned to usher everyone to the patio. Marcus and Jay were laughing and talking as we walked up. "Marcus, Porsche and Davarious are here. I don't think you officially met Davarious since Porsche tries to keep him locked up!" Porsche pushed my arm.

Marcus and Davarious shook hands. Marcus proceeded to introduce Davarious and Jay. Davarious said, "Shawn?" Jay gave a brief stare and said, "Naw man, Jay, good to meet you."

Davarious had a look on his face as if he was trying to solve a puzzle. "Man, you look just like a cat I knew back in the day. Y'all could be brothers on the real. He was much slimmer, but you resemble non-the-less. Anyway, good to meet you."

"Aw Davarious, is it? Nah man, I'm not from here. Don't have much family either. Maybe I've got a twin somewhere."

Davarious kept staring and said, "Yeah, maybe. I guess it's true, everyone has a twin."

Marcus was about done grilling the steaks and I set the table. Porsche and I were like two little girls at a sleepover. Giggling, smiling, and whispering about nothing. I didn't realize how much I missed my girl. We finally ate and had a variety of conversations from sports to politics. That's what I loved about Porsche. She was just as well-rounded as me. We could kick it with the guys but knew how to remain sophisticated at the same time.

I couldn't help but notice Davarious cutting his eyes at Jay throughout the evening. It was like he wanted to say something but didn't want to cause confusion. I don't know, I don't think anyone paid too much attention especially after the alcohol kicked in. Jay played it smooth most of the evening. I was so glad; he didn't try any slick shit. I'm keeping my fingers crossed in hopes he takes his ass to Japan.

Marcus and Jay began talking about work. We listened for a bit, but to be honest; we didn't want this to turn into a boardroom meeting, so I elected to put on music to lighten the mood. As I headed out of the kitchen Davarious asked where the bathroom was. Before I could answer; Porsche said, "Let me show you babe."

"Look y'all better not be trying to get freaky in my bathroom." We all laughed as Porsche grabbed Davarious by the hand leading the way.

Davarious had an awkward look as they got down the hall. He turned to Porsche and spoke.

"Yo babe. I know that dude from somewhere. He looks just like Shawn. I mean he's definitely older and been working out, but that's Shawn, it has to be him."

"Sweetheart, he said you were mistaken. Like y'all said, everyone has a twin somewhere. Besides, where do you think you know him and why would he say his name is Jay if it's Shawn?"

"Look, all I know is I knew this dude's name is Shawn from back in the day and that is him. I don't know what games he is playing or who he is hiding from, but that's Shawn all day long."

"I think you're overreacting, and you didn't say how you knew him."

Davarious looked down at the floor. "Babe, you know I had a past. I did a little time in Juvenile and this dude was in the bunk down the hall. They claimed his sister did some foul shit, fucked over this big-time dealer and he took the wrap for her. They tried to break him, but he wasn't budging. He did the whole bid. From Juvey' to Gen Pop. He was quiet but was not to be messed with. I remember once some little dudes tried to jack him for some damn shoes and the next day that man's throat was slit ear to ear. He made a real name for himself."

"Well, I think you're too focused on him and not enough on me." Porsche leaned in to kiss Davarious but stopped in her tracks as Dee yelled at them to hurry up.

"Y'all come on now, stop the freak show; we're ready to play drunkin charades."

Marcus and Porsche knew how much I loved playing Charades. Especially when drinking was involved. For every wrong guess, a shot was taken. The game didn't take long before everyone was laughing at everything. As everyone got more comfortable; I began to be more relaxed and less worried about Jay and anticipating his antics. We were having such a good time; I really didn't pay much attention as Jay kept egging Marcus on to drink more and more. After a few games; Porsche looked at her watch and looked surprised. "Girl, I didn't realize it was this late. Davarious and I have to go. We are heading out of town tomorrow. Do you need any help cleaning up?"

She looked at Marcus leaning in the chair. "Dee, is he going to be alright?"

I smiled as I watched him lay back as if no one else was in the room. Even though I've never seen him like this, I figured since we were home; he deserved to let his hair down.

"Girl, I got it. Yes, he'll be okay. I'm going to let him sleep it off right here on this chair. I'm so glad you came by." I walked them to the door, and we did our goodbyes. I turned around and there I saw Jay standing near the kitchen.

I took a deep breath and said; "Well, we're going to turn it and I've got to clean up and help get Marcus to bed."

"What's the hurry? I can help clean you up. Your man ain't going nowhere. I made sure of that."

"What the hell you mean; you made sure of that?" As I look over at Marcus, he was slouched even further in the chair. I called his name to make sure he was breathing. "Marcus, Marcus!" I was in panic mode.

"Oh, he's breathing, and he'll be fine. As a matter of fact, he won't remember half this night, but I bet you will…"

Before I could wrap my mind around what he said, he rushed towards me and put his hand over my mouth. I initially started to struggle, but oddly I wanted him even more than before. As he began to kiss me, he picked me up and sat me on the counter. He grabbed a switchblade from his pocket and slit my blouse as easy as slicing through warm butter. I was frozen with excitement and fear at the same time. As he kissed my breast and sucked my nipples; I began to shake with anticipation. I totally forgot about my surroundings. It was just me and this mystery man. A man I knew nothing about, yet he seemed to know my deepest desires and sexual needs.

This thang started to throb as if she had a heartbeat of her own. I heard his belt buckle hit the marble floor as his pants dropped. As quickly as his pants dropped, I felt the thick, warm manhood push inside me. I almost screamed with pleasure, but he grabbed around my throat with just enough pressure to quiet my pants of passion. We simultaneously exploded as he collapsed in my breast. As quickly as I exploded, my thoughts of passion and pleasure dissipated as reality hit. At that point, I wanted to fall to my knees and sob.

As he looked in my eyes and I could have sworn a look of regret came over him. But as fast as regret came, it receded as he looked back towards the living room and spoke.

"Don't worry, he'll be fine in the morning. I trust this will be our little secret. I mean you don't want to mess up this lavish life you have do you?"

He laughed as if he was in a comedy show. I couldn't believe it. What have I done? What type of person is my husband dealing with? If I tell Marcus, I'll have to tell what happened before. I can't tell Porsche. I have no one.

As he walked to the door, he boldly stepped over Marcus' legs as if he were taunting him. I ran and pushed it tightly and locked it as fast as I could. I ran to Marcus, and he was still breathing and seemed to be sleeping like a baby. I couldn't call the police; I couldn't do anything. I mean what would I say? "I'd like to report having an affair in my home with the man who spiked my husband's drink?" That's laughable. I wondered what and when he could have spiked Marcus' drink.

I mean we were all there! I ran to the shower, slid down the wall and started to cry like a newborn baby. I gathered the items of clothing including the ripped blouse and frantically stuffed them in the hamper. I'll get rid of the blouse when Marcus goes to work. How did my life turn into this? I don't know who I am anymore.

# 18

## Davarious

"I don't care what anyone says, that's Shawn's ass. I know that man. Man, we were in D County Detention together. I don't know what he's trying to do but that's him. Back then, he was a scrawny lil guy, but he wasn't scared by a long shot. I heard he and his sister did some real foul shit and fucked over some King Pin's money. I don't know what happened, but I heard it wasn't good. I was about to leave D County when he arrived, but none-the-less, I heard stories about him.

Yeah, he was a really skinny dude back then. Looks like he's done well for himself, but that's Shawn. I'm good with faces and that's him. I wonder why he pretended not to know who I was talking about? Shit, I guess if I had a past like I heard he had, I would want to forget too. He just seemed a little suspect though. He was quite standoffish with me the other night. Oh well, fuck it. Do what he do, just don't try to make me think I'm crazy when I'm not. Hell, I probably won't see him anymore. I don't hang around people like that anyway."

*Porsche walked into the room while Davarious was sitting on the side of the bed staring in space.*

"Babe, what are you thinking about? My big diamond ring?"

"Naw Baby don't worry about that. I've got that in the bag."

"Ooookaaay, don't go getting me some ghetto as ring from the Pawn Shop!"

"You mean to tell me you don't want one of those $59.99 his and hers sets?"

Laughing, Porsche pushed Davarious back on the bed and sat on his chest.

"You bet not bring me no shit like that!"

Davarious laughed while flipping Porsche over.

"I told you when I make you Mrs. Winston; you're only going to have the best."

# 19

## Jay

The other night was almost fucked by Davarious. Hell yeah, I remember his ass. Fuck, I didn't forget any of them wanna be hard motherfucka's in that place. I really can't say too much bad about him. I wasn't banking on running into anyone like that in little Ms. Dee's circle. She's too damn prissy. At least that's what she wants people to think. I knew I could bring out her inner skank. Hell, after I found out Marcus was the only one who hit that? Shiiiitttt, I knew what I needed to do. Curiosity killed the cat and that's just what I did, killed it!

A woman like that may look like she got her shit together on the outside, but her ass was curious, and I knew just how to lay it on thick to bring out that inner hoe. Fuck, she ain't had nothing, but one dick?! I knew Marcus' old ass wasn't giving her what she needed. I had to show her how the big boys roll. I've got to admit though, baby girl's shit was on point but a brother like me can't get lost in the sauce. I've got one mission and one mission only and nothing and nobody will get in the way of that.

Now, back to Davarious' ass. My gut tells me his ass may pose a problem and I can't have that. I waited all this time and nothing's going to stop what I started. That's for damn sure. The best thing for Davarious to do is forget he ever saw me if he knows what's good for him.

# 20

## Marcus

Man, I don't know what happened last night. If I didn't know better, I would think I was drugged. Hell, I can barely raise my head. I haven't drunk like that in years so, I guess I overdid it. I'll have a drink or two at dinner meetings, etcetera but to just straight drink and get drunk? I haven't done that since I was in my early twenties.

"Dee? Dee?" Man, where is my wife? And why did she leave me on this couch?

Dee ran down the hall in panic and wrapped her arms around Marcus.

"Marcus, are you okay? Baby I was so scared, you barely moved at first. I was able to get you to the couch from the chair, but I couldn't go any further. I haven't seen you like this before. What happened?"

"I don't know. You know I barely remembered anything after coming in from the patio. How's everyone else? I hope I didn't make a fool of myself, did I?"

"You could never do that! Everyone was fine. I noticed you drifting off to sleep, so I ended the night early and had everyone leave."

*As soon as Dee said that she became overwhelmed with guilt for what she had done. She mumbled; "Everyone except...". If I keep this up, I'll give myself away. I need to get it together.*

"Dee, did you say something? What's wrong? Are you sure I didn't do anything embarrassing? You look so sad."

"Babe, I'm tired that's all. We had a long evening and I had to clean up everything since you decided to take an early nap!"

We both laughed as I got up to shower.

"You know, I'm sure glad we didn't have to work today. Porsche's guy seemed cool. I would say we can do this again soon, but I don't think we'll be doing that again for a while."

"I agree. I'll fix you something to eat and have it ready when you get out of the shower. How does that sound?"

"That'll be great! And Dee? Thanks for being such a wonderful wife."

I jumped in the shower and the cool water seemed to wake me right up. I just can't shake this feeling that something ain't right. I've never drank like that and if I didn't know any better, I would think someone slipped me a Mickey, but I know damn well no one is bold enough to do something like that. Besides, who would? Why would they? I've done some pretty foul shit in my past, but that's ages behind me and no one around me knows my past. I made sure of that. Shit, Tammy's hoe ass is the only one who knew me from back in the day and I got that sowed up. She ain't going to say nothing. She knows better. I shook off the idea of being drugged and stepped out of the shower.

The cool air hit my body and I decided to lay across the bed and air dry. As I laid there, snippets of last night began to flash here and there. Shit after dinner and the first game of Charades, it was O-V. I can't remember shit. This is going to mess with me. I decided to get up and put my clothes on. I walked back to the bathroom and noticed I left my clothes on the floor. The least I can do is pick up after myself. Dee always takes such good care of me. She's one in a million I know that for sure. I opened the hamper and noticed Dee's blouse from last night.

"Hmph, that's strange. Dee never puts dry cleaner clothes in this hamper. Well, after the time she had with me, she probably dropped everything wherever she could. She said I didn't embarrass myself. I sure hope she's not trying to help me save face."

Dee walked in with a plate of food.

"Aw, thank you babe. Oh, by the way, I noticed your blouse in the hamper. You may want to grab it and put it with the clothes to be picked up for dry cleaning."

Instantly, Dee started to tense up. She just knew the jig was up.

"Oh, uh yeah. I'll get it. You know what babe; I have to run to the city, so I'll drop off the clothes instead of having them picked up. I promised to meet Porsche to help her with some ideas for her wedding."

Marcus sat there disappointed. He looked at Dee with sadness and said; "I thought you were going to take care of your man today."

"I know babe, but Porsche called while you were in the shower. It shouldn't take long. I'll be back in a few hours."

# 21

# *Dee*

I had no intention of going to the dry cleaners, nor had I talked to Porsche. Porsche hadn't even started any planning for her wedding. Lies. Lately, lies seemed to roll off my tongue with no remorse. I decided to go to the office and do a little work to clear my head. I just needed to get away from home. Being around Marcus made me more anxious and I was so afraid he would see right through me. I wish I could confess my soul and Marcus would see that I was taken advantage of and forgive me. Who am I kidding? As much as I hated what I did, I couldn't help but admit that I enjoyed the thrill of it all.

I knew this could only lead to a path of destruction, but I couldn't help but be intrigued. It felt like Jay tapped into this hidden part of my sexual being that craved the thrill of the unknown. The dangerousness of it all. Am I stupid? What would Porsche think? Shoot, I know what she would say. That's why I haven't told her. I can definitely see how some women get caught up, but I'm better than this. I know what's important and sins of the flesh can never trump true love.

My thoughts were interrupted as my phone vibrated. It was an unknown number. My first thought was to ignore it, but I didn't want to miss an important client.

"Hello, this is Dee Hampton-Alexander."

"Hello, Dee Hampton-Alexander. I'm sorry I didn't get a chance to give you a wake-up call. I know you slept well last night."

"Who is this?"

"Aw now, come on Dee. You should know my voice by now. I mean after last night; you know a lot more about me."

"What are you doing calling me? How did you get my number?"

"Is how I got your number your main worry? That should be the least of your concerns. How did hubby sleep?"

"He is absolutely fine and again how did you get my number and why are you calling me?"

"I just want to see how you were feeling. You seemed a little worried when you walked into the office earlier."

As soon as Jay uttered those words, an eerie feeling went all over my body. This fantasy is starting to turn into a nightmare. I looked around the office trying to trace my steps in my mind, wondering when and how long he had followed me. I started to feel this huge lump in my throat as I sat in my chair in disbelief. I couldn't show any signs of fear, so I tried to clear my throat to eliminate any possible tremble in my voice.

"I'll ask one last time. HOW THE FUCK DID YOU GET THIS NUMBER? WHY ON EARTH ARE YOU CALLING ME?"

Jay let out this taunting, cunning laugh. "Ms. Dee, it wasn't hard to get your number. Your precious Marcus always has his phone announce the name and numbers of his callers. Well, when *WIFEY* called, I just made a mental note of the number. You know you two deserve one another. You're both so damn smart and stupid as fuck at the same time."

I couldn't believe what I was hearing! I don't get it, I don't understand.

"Look, what do you want? You really need to leave me alone. As a matter of fact, you don't know who you're messing with Jay. I know people who could ruin you. You need to back the fuck off!"

"Hmph, I need to back the fuck off huh? Too bad you weren't saying that at the restaurant and YOUR HOUSE BOTH TIMES! I'll back off when I'm ready to back off and you and Marcus will know when I'm ready."

*Sheer panic went all over my body at the thought of Marcus finding out about us.* "You leave Marcus out of this! What did he ever do to you?"

As soon as I said that Jay was instantly quiet. It was like the phone shut off. I sat there as my heart started pounding so hard and so fast, I could feel the pulse in my temples. Suddenly, Jay's sardonic, condescending tone left, and sounds of mischief and rage emerged. Ignoring my question, he said;

"How do you think your husband would feel knowing you fucked his business partner? How do you think he would feel if he knew you let me taste you the first day I walked into his house? Do you think he would be happy to know his loving wife is no more than a two-bit hoe?"

At this point, I was doing everything not to pass out. I was without a doubt in the Twilight Zone. This kind of stuff doesn't happen to me.

"Stay away from me or else you won't have to worry about telling Marcus, I will tell him myself!"

"If only you believed that. You're not going to do that. Like I said Ms. Dee, I know more about you and yours than you do."

And just like that, he ended the call. By this time, I was so nervous, I didn't realize Porsche called me twice. I looked at the clock and realized I had been at the office for two and a half hours. I need to call Porsche. This is one situation I can't handle alone. I have never had to deal with or have experience with stalkers or crazy men. Porsche is my best friend; she'll know what to do. Besides, If I can't tell her, then who can I tell.

I couldn't focus on any of the files on my desk, so I decided to grab two folders to bring home just in case I needed proof of my whereabouts after I supposedly left Porsche's place. I walked out of the building paranoid; then instantly it dawned on me, I still never found out how he knew I was at the office. I cautiously walked to my car and looked around as I stepped in. I immediately called Porsche as I was pulling off the lot.

"Hi Porsche, do you have a moment today? Can I come by?"

"Dee, did you forget? Davarious and I are going out of town in just a few moments. Wait a minute; Dee you don't sound right? What's going on?"

"Oh yes, that's right I forgot. I'm sorry girl. You and Davarious can go ahead. I'll be okay."

Porsche could hear the anxiety in my voice. She huffed; "Naw now if you ain't aight; I ain't aight. What's the deal?"

Suddenly out of nowhere, I heard this horn blowing frantically. I totally ran straight through a traffic light! The next thing I know, my car was spinning around in the opposite direction. I wrestled with the steering wheel like I was fighting for my life. As my tires screeched and the smell of rubber burned, my car finally came to a stop. I was so afraid to move. I couldn't think, I was frozen with fear. All I could hear was Porsche screaming my name through the car speakers. I raised up and just as I turned to drag myself out of the car; the airbag deployed hitting me on the side of my head. The next thing I know, I woke up in Baylor Medical with Marcus and Porsche at my bedside. Marcus was holding my left hand and Porsche was holding on to my right arm as if she were holding for dear life. Although I had a horrible headache, I smiled when I saw them at my side. As the doctor walked in, Marcus began to bum-rush her with questions.

"Doc, how is she? What did the x-ray show? Is there internal damage? How long will she be here?"

I squeezed his hand to get his attention. "Marcus, please one thing at a time. Please let doctorrrr… I'm sorry, doctor, I don't know your name."

She gave me such a comforting smile; I knew I would be alright.

"I'm Dr. Pierce. You took a nice bump on the head, but all your tests were fine. You'll certainly be sore for the next few days, but overall, you'll be okay. We want to keep you for a few hours until your blood pressure comes down. Your husband told me you had no blood pressure issues and you're pretty healthy, so it's probably elevated due to the excitement. I'll leave you to rest and check on you later."

"Thank you, Dr. Pierce."

The doctor left as Marcus jumped to kiss my forehead. As soon as I looked up, Jay walked in with a water picture! I immediately felt lightheaded and sick. Marcus motioned for Jay to come closer. I know damn well this MOFO didn't come in here after what he did earlier. Why and how did he know we were here? I tried to ignore Jay's presence.

"Babe, how did you and Porche know I was here?"

Porsche jumped in and answered before Marcus could part his lips.

"Girl, you know we were on the phone and all I heard was crashing and noise. I immediately called Marcus. He said you two have that tracking shit on your phones, so he was able to find your location."

Damn, I forgot about that. I never used it, so I didn't think any more about it. Marcus jumped in and added…

"Yeah babe. And it was a coincidence, Jay happened to be coming out of the coffee shop and saw all the commotion. He saw your car and called me too! It was a great thing he happened to be there."

I did all I could not to roll my eyes and cuss this Fucka out while he was standing there with that slick look on his face.

"Oh yeah baby, great coincidence. You know I'm a bit tired, I just want to rest for a while if you don't mind. I appreciate you all so much. I really do."

"Okay dear heart. We'll let you rest, but I'm not leaving your side. By the way, do you know what happened? The police said it looked like you ran a traffic light."

Porsche noticed the look on my face. I could tell she knew something wasn't right and it was more than me being tired from the fender bender. Porsche interjected.

"Man, let the girl rest. Y'all can deal with that bullshit later. Marcus can you and Jay run to the cafeteria or something. I need my moment with my girl before I leave."

Marcus walked towards Jay and turned to look back like he was struggling to leave my side. "Y'all women are something else. Yeah, ok, but you know I'll be back. Yo Jay, you wanna take a stroll with me. Looks like I'll be taking a few days off to make sure Dee is okay and I need to give you some updates on some meetings we have with a new client. I'll be dialing in, but you know there's nothing like having competent representation in the flesh."

Marcus and Jay walked towards the door. Jay looked back and said, "Mrs. Xander, uhhh Alexander, take care of yourself."

I closed my eyes and didn't bother to respond as they walked away. When I thought they both cleared the doorway, I turned to Porsche with tears in my eyes.

Porsche grabbed a tissue to catch the tear that was a millisecond away from dropping down my face. "Girl, it's going to be okay, no one was seriously hurt. The other driver didn't get a scratch from what I heard. But that's not what's bothering you, is it? Come on with the come on. You don't like that Jay dude, do you? I saw you. Has something happened? I thought y'all were all cool and singing kumbaya and shit. You can hide it from Marcus, but you can't hide shit from me. What's the tea?"

I know Porsche was trying to make me smile with the kumbaya stuff, but the only thing I could do is bury my head further in the hard ass hospital pillow as the tears flowed.

"I just, I don't know how… he's just not a good person to be around. I don't have a good feeling about him."

Although I trusted Porsche with my life, I couldn't bring myself to tell her what I did. I couldn't admit to myself who I have become. This is no one's fault but mine. My life was perfect.

"Dee, look you ain't gotta say nothing you ain't ready to say. Focus on feeling better and you know I'm your girl through thick and thin."

At that moment, I realized Porsche was here with me and had not left to go out of town.

"Oh Porsche! YOUR TRIP WITH DAVARIOUS! And you're here with me I'm so sorry, you are supposed to be gone."

"Dee don't worry about that. Trips can be postponed. Being here with my bestie when she needs me the most, cannot. Ohhhh, speaking of Davarious. You know I never told you, but he thinks he knew Jay from somewhere. He said Jay didn't seem to know who he was talking about, but even so, he thinks he knows him. I only got an opportunity to see him that night at your house and I haven't heard Tammy mention him again not that I hear from her much. It's almost like he dropped in out of thin air. Hmmm, come to think of it, Davarious was adamant he knew him. He kept saying something about Shawn or something like that. Well, enough about him. Let me know what you need and when you need it, and I'm there. If you need a listening ear, a good cussing, or a partner in crime, I got you!"

We looked at one another and laughed. As Porsche prepared to leave, we said our goodbyes. We both knew without speaking there was so much more to say.

# 22

## Porsche

As I left the hospital, I couldn't help but think about my conversation with Davarious and about the look Dee had on her face when she saw Jay. I don't know what the deal is, but something is up with him. He didn't seem too cordial that night at Dee's. As a matter of fact, he appeared to be a little uptight to me. I mean, he's a handsome dude, but he seemed a bit arrogant. It was almost like he wanted to be way more important than he was. Or at least, that's what he wanted everyone to think. I've seen those types of men. They look like they got everything together and be just as fucked up as everyone else.

All I know is from the look Dee gave him, he better tread lightly. I still have my hood card in my back pocket. I'd hate to have to get someone to fuck him up! Well, I'm sure if it's something, Dee will tell me when she's feeling better. She sure seemed off-kilter. That's not like her. She's always calm and collected and thinking two steps ahead. Maybe she was shaken up from the wreck.

I called Davarious to let him know I was headed home. He was very understanding although I know he made plans for this trip a while ago. That's one thing I love about him. He always puts my concerns first and he doesn't get upset about every damn thing. It is so refreshing to deal with someone with no secrets! No moods swings, isolation, none of that shit. Lord, I couldn't have done better. THANK YOU!

I pulled up to the apartment building and handed my keys to the valet. As I walked in, I saw a couple getting on the elevator. The older man looked back, smiled, and graciously held the door as I rushed in. As I smiled at both of them and said thank you, his wife of whomever she was didn't even try to crack even a fake smile. Hell, I don't want her damn man. That old geezer, please. If I were a bitch, I would have made her really mad, but I don't have time to test her ignorance today. We came to the 15th floor, and I stepped off. I looked back at the gentleman, gave the most seductive smile, and said,

"Thank you again for waiting for me." He started to smile, but she cut her eyes at him so hard, he just nodded and looked away. She looked like she wanted to spit fire! I just couldn't help it. I had to be a little petty today. Females can be so damn insecure. Young and old.

I walked down the hall to my apartment and as I opened the door, Davarious was standing there with a beautiful ring. Hell, I was almost blinded by the glare of the diamonds. A man was standing with him and I thought I recognized him from some of his family pictures, but I was too focused on the ring to even care about who he was.

"Davarious, what is this? What's going on?"

"I told you, when I decide to make you Mrs. Winston, you will get the best."

"Mrs. Winston! But we said…"

"I know what we said, but I have my uncle here who is an Ordained Minister. Marry me now. We can have family and friends later. Besides, we are the ones who really matter. So, will you? Will you marry me?"

I wanted to snatch that ring and jump his bones right then and there. I hugged him so tightly, I could have bruised his ribs! "Oh, of course, I will and you know this man!"

We were married right there in my living room, and it was the most romantic evening I've ever had. He pulled out all the stops. He had a chef prepare dinner and a server. He took such good care of me, I felt like I was dreaming. I said to myself; "Porsche, you ain't ever letting this man go."

We stayed in for a week. We made love, ate, laughed, talked, shared our dreams and goals. I was so happy, but I felt bad, I forgot to check on Dee. She hadn't even called either. I'm sure Marcus is doting over her anyway. Davarious walked into the bedroom and said  his uncle and a few of his cousins wanted to help celebrate this new phase in his life.

"Babe, the fellas want to hang out a little and congratulate me on the nuptials. I was thinking I would kick it with them for a few hours and head back in. But I can just stay in another week with you."

Davarious moved closer to me and started to get back in bed. As much as I loved our week together, I know we must do other things and not neglect our family and friends forever.

"No sir, you go and celebrate. I'll be here when you get home. That will give me a chance to check on Dee."

"You haven't checked on Dee? Well, what kind of friend are you Mrs. Winston?"

"The kind that has been enjoying the love of her life. Dee understands. You be safe. Love you much!"

As Davarious left, I realized he didn't mention where they were going. Oh well, it's no big deal. I'll just get up and tidy up a bit. I can't let my husband think I don't keep house. MY HUSBAND! That sure sounds good.

# 23

## Jay

Marcus yapped on and on about the meeting with the clients and how he was going to dial into the meeting since he couldn't be there in person. He has always thought he was the shit. Don't nobody need his ass. He's too fucking arrogant to realize his bitch almost shit herself when she saw me walk into that hospital room. He really thinks he got that thing on a string. And Dee, talking all that shit like she was going to tell him herself. Her weak ass ain't going to do anything. I know her type. All talk but will bow down in a corner if you look like you going to come at her.

*This dude trusting me with his meetings, his company, his bitch! This is easy. It's almost too damn easy.*

My thoughts were interrupted by a call from my partner who owns the spot in Uptown Park. He is thinking about expanding and wanted to run a few ideas by me. It was the same spot I met Tammy, but the good thing about it was he wanted me to come by Saturday. She always showed her ass there on Thursday nights. She hit the most ratchet spots on Saturdays, so I didn't have to worry about running into her.

Hell, I haven't seen her since that night I used her to put Marcus on his P's & Q's and make Dee jealous. She called a few times and I ignored her for the most part. I did talk to her once and she asked what the deal was. She slickly tried to offer me some ass, but I didn't want any parts of that! I KNOW where that bitch has been.

I arrived at the club and just like clockwork, the owner had my special booth laid out with Remy on the table. We didn't waste any time talking about his expansion plans and advertising ideas. The meeting was going well when I looked up and saw a group of old heads walk in and be seated. They were a little loud and obviously celebrating something. I noticed Davarious was in the group, and it looked like they were celebrating whatever was going on with him. I guess the club owner noticed how I scowled at their table, and he called my name.

"Yo Jay. Man, you know them cats? Ain't going to be no shit is it?"

Realizing how I must have been looking, I tried to soften my grimace-filled face. "Naw man. I don't know them. The noise just threw me for a bit. You know your spot ain't usually that loud."

"Yeah, they made some last-minute reservations. One of them got married or some shit like that."

"Oh, no doubt. Maybe you can send a bottle to the table or something."

"Man, what? How about OR Nothing."

We both laughed. I noticed Davarious getting up and going to the bar. I kept my eye on him as I kept talking. "Man, advertisement remember? You send them something as appreciation for their business; they'll tell more people about your spot."

"Always the businessman huh."

"24/7! Look man, I'm going to help you out a little tonight. I'm going to the bar, and I'll send something over. On me. I'll be right back."

Davarious was sitting at the bar looking at the beer and wine menu when I sat down. I grabbed a menu knowing damn well I already knew what I was going to order. I want to make sure he's not going to be a thorn in my fucking side.

Davarious looked up. I could tell by his demeanor he knew who I was. I know he knew exactly who I was a few weeks ago. Davarious turned to me and said, "Jay, is it?"

"Yeah man or Shawn's twin whatever you want to call me."

"Twin huh. Aight man. I don't know what game you are playing or who you may be running from, but I know you, Shawn. It ain't my business though. As long as it doesn't affect me and mine, I'm straight. You stay out of my way, and I'll stay out of yours."

"Me and mine? Oh, the celebration is for you? Well, congratulations D, my man. Congrats. Do your thing. Trust me, as long as you and yours don't fuck with what I got working, y'all good."

Davarious stood up from the chair as if he were a soldier getting ready for battle. I know he had hands back in the day, but he doesn't want any of this. He just doesn't know.

"Well, me and mine includes anyone close to my wife. So don't try me. You know me SHAWN!"

The bartender looked confused as he moved closer after he heard Davarious' voice. "Yo Jay my man, everything good?"

I waved for the bartender to go back to his duties. "Oh yeah man. Me and D-man just having a little chat. Send some of the best wine to his table on me." I turned my attention back to Davarious.

"Like I said, if you and yours stay in your place, then you're good. And by the way, the name's Jay. I don't know a Shawn. Man, you should really let that go."

I strolled away from the bar back to my booth where the owner was waiting. I knew then and there, Davarious was going to be a pest and I needed to exterminate. I let the bar owner finish up his little spill and told him I had to think about things. I knew damn well; I was going to go for the idea. It was a surprisingly good pitch, and I was already invested in his business so anything to make additional money was good with me. I sat there long enough to watch Davarious and his table of flunkies. As people from his table began to leave one by one, I watched until only Davarious and some old dude were left. I told the owner I was leaving. I went through the kitchen and departed from the back door by the receiving office. I made it to the alley in the back just in time enough to see Davarious leave.

I jumped into my Challenger and zipped down the highway behind Davarious. I kept enough distance so he wouldn't notice me tailing. He exited onto Elm Street and I sped past two cars to make sure I didn't miss the exit as well. He parked on the side of the building and ran into the store. I zipped around and parked on the opposite side of this old van that probably belonged to some construction workers or something based on the ladder and tools I noticed. He came out with a key attached to a sign and went to the restroom located outside the store. I ran and pulled on the door knowing it was a long shot that it would be open. No one could be that dumb. I'll be damned, my lucky night, it opened…

Davarious kept his back turned while yelling; "Ay man, someone's in here. Be out in a minute."

Before he could turn around, I grabbed my switchblade from my pocket and slit his ass from ear to ear. He didn't get an opportunity to see my face, but I made sure that muthafucka heard me. As he slid to the floor grabbing his throat, I uttered the last words he would ever hear.

*"Is this your way of protecting you and yours?"*

As he lay in a pool of blood, I grabbed some paper towels, wiped the door handle, and darted out that bitch like the grim reaper himself.

## 24

*Porsche*

It's 4 am! Where the hell is Davarious? We haven't been married but a good week and he's already with this bullshit! If he thinks I'm one of these females who's going to put up with this kind of disrespect, he's got another thing coming. What he's not going to do is stroll in and out of this house at all times of the night. He didn't do that when we were dating, so I don't understand why he thinks he can do it now. I've called his ass nine damn times and the phone initially just rang; now it's going to voicemail like the phone is off. I don't want to be one of those crazy wives calling around for her man, but if he doesn't answer in the next 10 minutes; I'm going to call his uncle who he claimed he was going to meet. I don't give a damn if it is four in the morning; if I'm up, every damn body is going to be up.

As 5 am approached, I decided to fix ME some breakfast. There was no reason why I should be mad on an empty stomach. I got up, brushed my teeth, and took a shower. And to think, I was lying here in my best lingerie thinking my man was going to come home to a treat and his ass hasn't even thought enough about me to call and make up a lie.

By the time I showered, fixed breakfast, and paced the floor over and over, it was 6 am. I turned on NBC 5 to watch Blakeney Stokes report on the overnight happenings in the area. I got up to pour another cup of coffee and noticed breaking news scrolling across the screen. I saw yellow tape behind the news anchor and thought to myself *"What now?"* while turning up the volume.

*"Good morning, this is Blakeney Stokes, reporting live at the gas station off Elm Street where we are being told an abandoned Dodge Charger and a body have been found. No name has been released; however, we do know the car is a 2015 black Dodge Charger. If anyone has information on this, we asked that you contact the authorities at the number scrolling across your screen. We will keep you updated*

*on any developments. This is Blakeney Stokes reporting live NBC 5 Dallas. Now back to you Krista."*

I stood frozen and the only thing that snapped me out of it was the sound of the coffee mug shattering on the floor! I immediately grabbed the phone again and feverishly dialed Davarious' number over and over. There's no way, it can't be his car, it just can't be.

After calling back-to-back for what seemed like twenty more times and getting voicemail; I finally thought to call Dee. She picked up on the third ring.

"Hello."

"Dee? Please I need…"

I was so hysterical I don't even know what I was saying. All I knew was my new husband hadn't come home, he wasn't answering his phone and the description of the car found on the news sounds like his.

"Porsche, wait a moment. Slow down. What's wrong?"

All I could do is scream and cry on the phone. I knew I wasn't making any sense, but I couldn't calm myself enough to tell her my worst fear.

"Dee, could you take me to the police station? Davarious hasn't come home, and I saw a car like his on the news. I don't know what to think, I'm so scared. What if?"

"Girl, without question. Let me wake Marcus up. We're on our way. Don't do anything until we get there. We'll get it sorted out. I'm sure everything will be fine."

"Okay."

I hung up the phone knowing damn well there was plenty to worry about. I felt it in my soul. Something's happened to Davarious. I knew he wouldn't just refuse to come home. That's not who he is. There has to be another explanation. He loves and respects me too much for that shit. I can't believe I ever thought he was playing games.

The 15 minutes it took for Marcus and Dee to pick me up seemed like hours. I'm sure I have a permanent trail on my kitchen floor from all the pacing back and forth.

Marcus came up to the apartment. He said Dee was waiting in the car and wasn't up to walking in. Damn, I forgot Dee was still sore from the accident. He was very comforting and encouraging. I tried to pretend he was making me feel better, but we both knew it wasn't working. It took all my strength just to make it the car. My legs felt like noodles, and I thought I would pass out at any moment. Marcus helped me into the car, and I immediately reached for Dee's hand for support and she already had her hand out waiting. The ride to the station felt like the longest ride of my life!

We arrived at the police station and as I walked in, my legs began the slide from underneath me. Marcus grabbed me and helped usher me in. There were two officers at the desk. The older lady looked like she had a chip on her shoulder. I was not in the mood for that shit, so I walked towards the middle-aged gentleman. He smiled and offered to assist. I tried to speak, but tears began to roll and my voiced trembled uncontrollably, so Marcus took over.

"Hello officer. My friend's husband has been missing since yesterday and the abandoned vehicle at the gas station mentioned on the news looks like his car. Is there someone in charge she can speak with?"

Before the young man could answer, the old bitch yelled over "If it's not been over twenty-four hours, you cannot file a missing person's report."

I wanted to jump across the counter and slap her but before I could, Marcus grabbed my shoulder to calm me and addressed her.

"And you're absolutely correct in any normal situation; however, in this case, there was a public plea to report if we had any information on the abandoned car or person. I believe this fits the criteria for what was asked. Now correct me if I'm wrong?"

The old officer looked like a lost puppy and shrugged her shoulders as she turned to walk away.

I had to get my two cents in, so I yelled; "Yeah, go file some papers and eat a donut wide back bitch!"

Marcus grabbed my hand, and the other officer shook his head at the lady as if to say he would handle our concerns. The young officer showed us to a private room and asked if we could wait for a moment.

Moments later, a detective walked in with a manilla folder in his hand. He proceeded to ask about the car and I gave him an accurate description. He sat down and wanted me to tell him about Davarious. He told me they found an ID in the car and a wallet at the scene. As I braced myself to look at the ID; all I could do is scream and ask why? Sure enough, it was

Davarious. I asked the detective what happened, and he gave me a somber look and asked if he had any enemies.

"Enemies? Noooo, Davarious wouldn't hurt anyone. What happened to him?"

The detective said I would need to ID the body before going into further detail to ensure it was Davarious. Marcus motioned for the detective to speak with him privately. They stepped outside the door while I was left to cry while holding Davarious' ID in my hand. They quickly returned and the detective said he normally would not go into detail until a positive ID of the body has been made, but in this case, he would make an exception. The detective took a deep breath, looked at me with so much compassion and said it looked like an act of revenge. He said there was nothing missing so they couldn't rule it as a robbery gone bad. He said from the looks of his injury, this was someone who knew him and wanted him to suffer. Then he looked at me and asked how long I had known him. At that point, I lost it.

"What the hell do you mean, how long have I known him? Long enough to be his wife that's how long. Look you find who the hell did this to my husband and why."

The officer gave his condolences and offered Marcus his card. He said if we could think of anything, give him a call no matter what time, day or night. I turned and said, "the only thing I can think of at this moment is how I need to plan a funeral for my new husband and walked away."

I looked at Marcus in disbelief and asked "Why? Who would want DAVARIOUS DEAD?"

# 25

## Marcus

That was messed up what happened with Davarious. And he and Porsche just got married? That's some vendetta type of shit for your ass. He seemed like a pretty cool dude, but he obviously had an enemy. Made me think about the kind of hits I used to order back in my day. Shitttt, back in the day I kept my distance from a police station. I sure as hell wouldn't have volunteered to go to one. It wasn't a big deal though, hell most of the PI's are long gone and half were on my payroll back then.

The drive back home was a somber one. Porsche crying one moment and, in a daze the next. Dee trying to hold her hand and be supportive. Man, what can you say in a situation like this? I used to order hits and didn't think twice about the impact on the person's family. All I thought about is someone crossed me or tried to cheat me, so I made sure they were dealt with in one way or another. Man, just looking at Porsche, I feel some sort of remorse for all the shit in my past. But one thing's for certain, you live, and you learn. I'm just thankful I had the chance to turn my life around and live long enough to reap some of the rewards of my hustle.

Porsche's going to need Dee's support right now and maybe that's a good thing. That'll keep Dee busy while I take care of this business. I always invite her to come to after-hours meetings, etc., because I promised myself the last thing I would do is make my wife feel second to my job. I dogged females for years and yeah it hunts me from time to time, but I've changed for the better and left that life behind.

If Dee knew anything about who I use to be, I know she would walk, and I can't have that. Yeah, I definitely think Dee should be there for Porsche's misfortune. That'll keep Jay from eyeing mine. I see the shit and it doesn't bother me because I know I've got mine sowed up, but I know men like Jay. I used to be Jay. Hungry to be on top. Wanting nothing but the best, pockets on swoll and a ride or die dime piece by my side. He's just a young cat though. He thinks he's getting by with the slick looks. He can look all day long, but he can't touch. I know my girl and it's going to take a lot more than some suit and job to impress her.

I'm glad my baby getting back to feeling better after the accident. I haven't asked her about what happened anymore, nor have I asked her about the look she gave Jay at the hospital. I caught that shit. I know this dude ain't stupid enough to try to make a play at mine. He definitely doesn't want to see the old me. Hell, back in the day; I wouldn't have given him a chance to look. He would have been done with the first glance. One thing's for sure, I know how to keep my friends close and enemies closer.

When we left the hospital the other week; Jay and I went over a few meeting topics. Since I couldn't be there in person, this would be the test to see if Jay could represent and walk the walk. I'm going to run the Japan idea by him again to see if he bites. After a few meetings with the Cuaq Coi Inc executives, we agreed the project wouldn't take as long to finalize; maybe a few weeks. As a matter of fact, I think I'll hit him up before we get back to Porsche's place.

"Hey Jay man. You got a moment."

"Sure man. What's up?"

"So, I spoke with Mr. Coi at Cuaq Coi Inc and we're thinking we can finalize everything in a few weeks."

Jay jumped to respond like he was waiting on me to offer him the deal.

"Aw Yeah? A few weeks?"

"Yeah man, three weeks or less if there are no hiccups in the contract. Dee and her friend got some disturbing news; I would like to stick around for a while. I was thinking you would like the opportunity to close this deal and make a real name for yourself in the company. How does that sound?"

You could almost hear Jay smiling through the phone.

"Oh yes, that would be great Marcus. No problem at all. When do I leave?"

"Whoa, whoa, slow your roll. There are a couple of things we need to cover here. In the meantime, I'll have the secretary start booking your flight and hotel stay. That cool?"

"Bet. Yo man. Thanks for this vote of confidence."

"Man, you've got this. We'll talk later."

"Oh yeah, and I hope Dee's better and everything's okay with Porsche."

"Okay, bet."

I hung up the phone and thought I didn't think I called Porsche's name. What would make him think I was talking about her? Hmph, maybe he figured since I said close friend, he assumed it was Porsche.

# 26

## Jay

This came right on time. It'll give me a chance to regroup and clear my head. I mean Davarious wasn't in the plan, but when you get in my way; you get fucked up. I can't believe that dude! He was talking big shit like he being a bad muthafucka. He really thought he was going to bitch me? Hell no; talking about not crossing him and his wife. Bullshit, I guess he learned the hard way, not to fuck with me.

I'm sure Dee was really pouring it on thick trying to take care of Porsche. She has this deep desire to feel needed and she'll stop at nothing to make herself feel relevant. (Taking a sip of Hennessy) Hmmm, perhaps I'll send flowers. Nah, I bet not. Hell, as far as I'm concerned it was just something unfortunate that happened to someone I met once at Marcus' house. That's my story and I'm sticking to it!

The secretary called me the next day with flight information and hotel reservations.

She said I would be flying first class with JAL from DFW airport. This is a FREAKING 13 HOUR FLIGHT! They better have something better than some damn peanuts and crackers on this damn flight. She was able to book a Deluxe King Room at the Sheraton Miyako Hotel. I won't be leaving for another week and a half, so I have time to put some things in place here. This should be pretty cool.

I'm going to do this little deal, get even more in Marcus' good graces and then go for the jugular. One thing's for certain and two things for sure. They will regret the day they ever crossed me and mine.

# 27

## Tammy

Shit, I heard through the grapevine Porsche lost her new hubby. Damn, that's fucked up. I would call her, but I don't know what the fuck to say. I've never been able to sound sincere with shit like that. Maybe because I've seen so much death and pain, it doesn't faze me much. The way a bitch like me thinks, if I didn't know any better, I would think Porsche set that shit up for the insurance money. I mean, they got married REAL quick. I didn't even know they were serious. Well, it ain't like females tell me much about their men anyway.

They're always intimidated by a bitch like me. I can't help if their men flock to me like flies to shit! Speaking of shit, I know one bitch who ain't got to worry about her man and that's Dee. Been there, done that and finally broke free? Hell, Marcus' little reformed roll ain't going to keep up. Sooner or later and I may very well be dead before it happens, but old Xander is going to show up again. A Pin that deep in the game can't let that shit go and no one can make me believe it.

I think I'm going to head out for the evening. I wonder which trick I'll get to take care of me tonight. Speaking of trick; I called Jay a couple of times after we went out. To tell the truth about it, he ain't got enough thug in him for me. I mean, he looks good and all, but he is a little too high maintenance for me. He seemed cool one minute and zoned out and moody the next. I've been around the block enough to know that niggah got some shit going on. I can't figure him out and really ain't trying to.

Yeah, I was going to let him sample this kitty, but he acts all serious and shit like he is looking for relationship material or something. That is definitely a no-no for me. The last time I called, he was talking all slow and shit. It doesn't take a rocket scientist to know we weren't vibing. Hell, like I said before, I think he wants Dee's ass. Shit, she would probably be better off if she knew who she was fucking with on the real.

I know one thing, if I don't ever run into Marcus's ass again, it will be too soon. The only place I want to see him is when we look across the room at each other while we are burning in hell. I would be okay with it knowing his low-down ass is there too.

I think I'm going to wait on going anywhere tonight. I'll just pour a glass of Henny and light up this loud and chill for the evening. I'll wait until Thursday night to turn up at my spot. I do need to relax and let my hair down. Hell, I ain't gotta worry about Jay being there and if his preppy ass is, I'll just turn up and let him see how a real woman parties. He'll be hating he passed up on this once-in-a-lifetime chance.

## 28

### Dee

I can't believe what happened to Davarious! And poor Porsche, she just found love and now her life has been turned upside down. I can't imagine what I would do if I lost Marcus. Things like this really make you put things into perspective. My heart aches that I cheated on him. I don't even want to think about *me and cheating* as one and the same. I am embarrassed and disappointed that I even let that happen. I think I may stay with Porsche for a few days. Helping her will give me a chance to focus on something else other than me and my mess. During the ride to Porsche's, I heard Marcus on the phone with Jay. I sure hope his ass goes away and gets lost. I don't care if he ever comes back. The further away, the better. We pulled up to Porsche's and we all just sat in the car for a moment. I mean what do you say at a time like this? Marcus broke the awkward silence.

"Dee let's get Porsche up to her apartment. Are you feeling well enough to make it up?"

In the midst of all Porsche's drama, I forgot about my little pain after the accident.

"Oh, yes. I'll be fine. I just want to make sure my girl is okay."

We stood outside the car for a moment waiting on Porsche to move. She seemed like a frozen statue. Marcus and I both motioned to escort her from the back seat. She stepped outside the car and leaned against it as if she had no energy left. She looked at me with tears in her eyes and said, "Dee, why? What could he have done to deserve this? Why would anyone hurt him?"

I reached out to hug her and she buried her head in my arms and almost collapsed to her knees. Marcus helped me pull her to her feet and we were able to direct her to the apartment. When we made it to the door, she attempted to get the keys from her purse and in a daze, she dropped her purse to the floor as she stared into space. I picked up her purse and got her keys. As I opened the door and walked in, there was a shattered mug on the floor. I started to clean it up and Porsche yelled; "JUST LEAVE IT! It doesn't matter, nothing matters." She began to sob even more. My heart ached for Porsche. I could see anger, hurt, despair, and confusion all wrapped into one. I looked at Marcus and we nodded in agreement like we both knew I needed to stay with her.

"Porsche, would you like for me to stay here with you?"

Through all the hysteria, she managed to pull herself together for a moment. All of a sudden, she had this look that I'd never seen before. Her eyes were glazed, and you could see pure unadulterated anger. "Why? Do you think you can help me by staying here? Can you bring Davarious back? Can you tell me why someone would KILL him? As a matter of fact, little *Miss My-Shit-Don't-Stank-ALWAYS-Got-It-Together-Dee,* since you have all the fucking answers; tell me why the only two men I ever cared about either left or died! CAN YOU TELL ME THAT? If you have the answer for that, then fine; stay. If not; GET THE FUCK OUT AND LEAVE ME THE HELL ALONE!"

Porsche grabbed a pillow and fell into the cushion of the couch and sobbed even more. I was shocked because she never clicked on me like that, and I tried to understand. I can't say that my feelings weren't hurt because they were. I couldn't help but think to myself; "Do I give off a vibe that my life is perfect?" That's surely not how I want to be seen, especially not by my best friend. I thought to myself *Out of hurt and anger; the truth will appear.*

I stood there next to Porsche for what seemed like a lifetime. I looked at Marcus with tears in my eyes and walked towards the door. Marcus grabbed my hand to reassure me. He stopped me from walking through the door and said, "She's hurting Dee. No matter what she said, she needs you. You can't leave her alone. Sweetheart, just give her some privacy but don't leave her. She loves you and you know it." Marcus told me he would grab some clothes from home and bring them back to me. He suggested that I stay the night and see how things look tomorrow to determine if I should stay longer.

As hurt as I was, I knew he was right. He kissed me on the head, told me to call if I needed him and closed the door. I quietly finished cleaning up the broken mug off the floor and put on some hot tea. I don't know what the hell tea will do at this time, but that was all I could think to do. I sat quietly in the gray high back swivel chair sitting in the corner of the room near the bookshelf. I watched Porsche like a hawk. The ebb and flow of her ear-piercing cries of despair and deep sobs of hopelessness moved across the room almost musically. I soon began to tune out the noise.

When all was quiet, I looked around the room and admired Porsche's collection of books. Her collection ranged from love & romance, criminal and even dark mythical stories. She loved to read, and it didn't matter what it was. I thumbed through the array of books and decided to read *Therapy Sessions by Marquisa Laflora*. If anyone needed therapy, I sure as hell did. I almost got through the first chapter when I heard Porsche's sobs change to whimpers as she called my name.

"Dee, I'm sorry. I didn't mean what I said. It's just that no matter how hard I try, how well I treat people; I always get the short end of the stick. I'm beginning to think I'm meant to be alone. First, it was Tye, then Davarious? What next?"

I felt helpless because as much as I wanted to, I didn't know how she felt. To be honest, I didn't want to know what she felt. I don't think I could handle it. "Porsche, it's okay. I understand. You do and say whatever you need to; I'm here for you."

Porsche stood up from the couch like she was ready to leap for joy… "See, that's what I mean. No matter what; you're there. Calm, cool and collected. I guess that's why you're a badass attorney and I'm the medical assistant who's failed the RN exam three fuckin' times! I've studied for that bitch so much; I could write the damn test! I only live comfortably now because of the money my dad left me."

For a second, we looked at one another and bust out laughing. She had taken the RN exam a few times. She knows her stuff, I just think she panics on the test. Even through the smiles and laughter, I couldn't help but recall the piercing words that seared my soul earlier. I wonder if she truly meant what she said. Porsche kept mentioning Tye & Davarious. I always wanted to ask Porsche what happened with Tye, but I didn't dare ask her; especially not at a time like this.

I went to the kitchen and decided to pour us a cup of tea. Porsche yelled into the kitchen, "If Remy ain't mixed in that tea, you can keep that shit in there!" I shook my head in laughter, but I decided to grab the bottle of Remy Martin from the bottom of the cabinet and mix a swig with the tea because I knew the girl wasn't playing when it comes to her Cognac.

We sat there for a while in silence as we sipped the spiked tea. Porsche would reflect on her time with Davarious and cry off and on. Before we knew it, the 9 o'clock news was on. A reporter came on and mentioned the unsolved case regarding

Davarious. I grabbed the remote to change the channel and Porsche asked me to leave it. I said, "Do you really think it's a good idea to sit here and watch this? Porsche, you need to try to relax."

Porsche obviously irritated, "Dee, do you think relaxing is something I can do right now? I mean really? I've still got to call his mother and make arrangements. I've never delivered that kind of news to anyone. How do I start? What am I supposed to say?"

I held Porsche's hand, "Well, you can't do anything tonight. Let me worry about the funeral arrangements and I'll be right here with you whenever you need to call anyone."

Porsche and I sat in silence, and I continued to watch her until she drifted off to sleep.

## 29

Two weeks had gone by and there were still no leads in Davarious' murder. Porsche tasked me with making all the funeral arrangements. She said she couldn't bear to do it. She said just tell me where and when and she would be there. I felt she needed to help with the arrangements in order to give her some sort of closure, but she refused. She did finally get the courage to let his family know about his passing and from that point, she handed the reigns to me. They didn't have an insurance policy yet, so Marcus and I decided to pitch and help with the services. I made the arrangements with Peaceful Rest. They were so helpful. Once I told them what I thought she wanted, they took care of everything else.

The service came and went. Porsche was there in body, but her mind was far away. She did say she didn't want a traditional repast. So, after the graveside service, everyone disbursed and went their separate ways. On the way to her apartment, she told me she just wanted to get some clothes and asked if it was okay if she stayed at our place for a couple of days. She said she couldn't bear to stay at the apartment with so many memories of Davarious there. Marcus was fine with it, so we stopped by her place and then headed home.

We arrived home and I prepared the other master suite. Marcus always thought we had too much room for just the two of us, but I knew the extra rooms would come in handy. Porsche would have her own bed, bath and a great view of the city. Initially, she stayed locked in her room and only came out when we forced her to eat. Needless to say, a couple of days turned into TWO DAMN WEEKS! She had taken a leave of absence from work, so she was there 24/7. She loved to lay on the Victorian chaise lounge and just stare out of the window.

Hell, I thought she was going to start sprouting roots on my damn furniture if she didn't get her ass up a do something. Don't get me wrong, I definitely want to be here for my girl, but at some point, she's got to snap back to the land of the living. Marcus seemed to be very patient, but my patience was dwindling slowly but surely. He was so busy with work; I don't even think he noticed how much of an inconvenience she had become. One evening I decided to have a talk with him about helping her get back to normal.

Marcus walked into the house, loosened his tie, and put down his briefcase. I figured I'd catch him before he got too comfortable. "Marcus, we need to talk. I want you to know how much I appreciate you letting Porsche stay here for a few weeks. I love how supportive you have always been but…"

Before I could finish, he stopped me and finished my thought.

"But it's time for her ass to go!" We both fell out laughing because, for the first time in weeks, we weren't tipping around worrying about making her feel comfortable.

I asked, "Babe, how long have you felt this way and why haven't you said anything?"

He said, "Dee, I know how much she means to you, so I wanted to be there as long as you needed me to, but to tell you the truth; I miss my alone time with my wife."

I looked at him and felt like I fell in love all over again. We started to kiss, and Porsche interrupted.

"Oh, I'll be out tomorrow. I was waiting on Marcus to get home so I could let both of you know how much I appreciated you, but I've overstayed my welcome. I guess I'm not the only one who felt that way."

MY GOD, she was standing there and listening the whole time. I felt so guilty for her overhearing us. I started apologizing…" Porsche, I'm sorry, we didn't mean for it to sound like that. We love you."

Porsche looked totally exasperated; "Girl, I know. It is what it is. If the shoe were on the other foot, I would have kicked your ass out a long time ago."

*We all tried to laugh, but deep down we knew her feelings were hurt.*

By the way, the detective called me and said he wanted to come by tomorrow and ask a few questions. I told him I would meet him at my house around 2 pm. Can either of you take me home this evening instead? I need to get used to being home alone again."

I turned to Marcus and asked, "Do you mind babe? You know I have this late conference call and I want to make sure I prepare."

Marcus looked at Porsche. "No problem, you, my girl. Let me know when you're ready to leave and we'll head out."

Just then, the doorbell rang. We looked confused because no one was expecting any visitors. Marcus got up from the couch and opened the door. It was JAY! I was speechless, I thought his ass was in Japan.

Marcus stepped back to let Jay in. "Man, long time no see. I thought you were going to be there another two weeks or so."

Jay walked in like he owned the place. "Yeah man, things went great! I had my meetings, pitched our ideas, and laid out the plan to have everything done in record time. When Mr. Coi saw how detailed and determined we were, he gave a hellified advancement and finalized everything! Man, you should have seen it. I had them eating out of the palm of my hands!" Suddenly he stopped and his excitement calmed. He looked at Porsche and me. "Hi Mrs. Alexander. Porsche, I heard about your loss. My condolences."

I barely mumbled hello and Porsche turned towards the hall and said, "Thanks, I guess."

Marcus told Porsche he needed to handle this business really quick as he was pouring Jay and his celebratory drink. Jay helped himself to a seat at our bar.

Porsche said, "Oh yeah, no doubt, handle your business. I'll be in the back. Dee, do you want to help me pack?"

Porsche had this look on her face as she kept cutting her eyes at Jay. I felt her discomfort and I don't know if she sensed mine or if there was something else going on. Porsche and I walked to her room and sat on the bed. She was folding clothes quietly and then broke her silence.

"Dee, it's something about him and I don't like it. Davarious kept telling me he knew him, but he claimed not to know him at all. He just looks sneaky. Something ain't right with his spirit, I feel it."

I sat there for a moment, and I don't know why the hell I did it, but I thought now was the time to bare my soul. "Porsche, he's not a good person. Not a good person at all. He's evil and conniving and I just want him gone."

Porsche could sense I was trying to tell her something. All of a sudden, her eyes got huge, and she looked at me like a mother scolding her child. "Dee, tell me you didn't? Bitch and you got this man all up in y'all's house!!! WHAT THE FUCK IS WRONG WITH YOU?"

My eyes were huge because of how loud she was and my fear of them overhearing us. "Shhhhhh, damn, what are you talking about? I just said he's not a good person."

"Look Dee, I've been around the block long enough to know when someone is not being straight up with me. You've been acting differently for months. And come to think of it, your ass be all jittery like when someone mentions him, or he comes around. Bitch I ain't stupid. You can fool your hubby with that shit, but you can't fool me. I've known you pretty much all your life. You foul Dee, that's foul."

At that point, I knew there was no reason to continue to lie to Porsche. My eyes filled with tears, and I hung my head in shame. "Porsche, I don't know what happened. And when I tried to end it, he said some of the most awful things to me. He even stalked me at my job. The day of the wreck, I was so upset because he called and followed me to work."

Suddenly Porsche stopped me; "Girl, stop. Now it all makes sense. The wreck, the hospital? How he just happened to be in the area. What the hell are you going to do? Look, I got you no matter what, but this is a dangerous game you're playing and you're playing with the devil."

Porsche started hitting me on my leg, "WHA-TA-MINUTE, WHAY -ONE- DAMN- MINUTE! How the fuck did he know Davarious died? Did Marcus say anything to him? I thought I heard him say he was out of the country. How long has he been gone?"

Porsche's wheels started turning like she was an investigator on First 48. Just then her phone rang. It was the detective handling Davarious' murder investigation. I tried to eavesdrop, but all I could hear was Porsche saying, "Really! Really! Then there's hope we may get some answers. Yes, I can meet today instead of tomorrow. Thank you so much."

Porsche hung up the phone and smiled like she had just won the lottery. She grabbed her purse and my hand and pulled me down the hall like we were in a race to the kitchen where Marcus and Jay were having a drink.

She yelled, "Marcus, I'm sorry to interrupt, but do you think you could take me home now? I just got a call from the detective. They found a partial bloody fingerprint at the scene and want to review a few more things with me! Isn't that great! This may be just the break we need."

Jay put his drink down and looked like he saw a ghost. I stood there, heart pounding from Porche snatching me up and dragging me down the hall. I got tickled for a moment. She's always been one strong ass Bitch.

Jay stood up and said, "Oh Marcus man, y'all go take care of your business. We can catch up on the office matters later." He walked to the door so fast, he didn't bother to wait for anyone to see him out.

Marcus walked to the door just in time to catch Jay before he darted out. "Yeah, man. We'll catch up later."

Porsche was right on Marcus' heels. After he closed the door she said, "I don't know what you like about that dude Marcus, something ain't right with him and I don't like him. Maybe he's a good businessman. Like my mom use to tell me, "Keep yo friends close and yo enemies closer. I know you better keep that muthafucka in yo damn pocket."

Porsche gave me a scolding look as if she were a mother chastising her child. I pretended not to know what the look was about. Marcus kissed me and they headed out to take Porsche home.

# 30

## *Jay*

Ain't this bout a bitch! I know I wiped down shit after slicing that bitch ass niggah throat. Hell, I tried my best to zip out that muthafucka like a fuckin ghost too. I know I didn't leave anything behind. Shit if they run that print, the way my ass so twisting up in the system, my shit is going to blow up like fireworks on the fourth of July. I know one thang, these muthafucka's fucked my life up once. I'll be damned if that happens again. I jumped into my car and waited down the street until Marcus and Davarious' Bitch left. I gotta do something with that THOT. I can tell, she may have a little more street smarts than her green-ass friend Dee. She seems nosey like her fucking dead ass husband. All I can say is if she wants to be a pest too, then call me the exterminator bitch.

I followed them to the apartment. Luckily, I was rolling a rental so Marcus wouldn't have quickly recognized me. I parked far away but close enough to see everything around me. I thought out loud, "this would be the perfect time to kill this muthafucka" and to knock her ass off would be a bonus. I could send her to see her husband quicker than she thought.

I was fantasizing so hard about getting rid of this niggah, I didn't realize the damn "Donut Muncher" had parked and was walking to the apartment building. Shit, I forgot that was the whole reason why I had to follow their ass here. I'm going to sit here and buy some time. Today may be the day ole Marcus meets his Maker. On the other hand, I better slide in to check out the scene. People were coming and going so I figured I would blend in well. I trotted to the door and made it just in time to see this Barney Fife-looking Po-Po get on the elevator. I walked to the Concierge and decided to try my luck to get her to give me Porsche's apartment number. She was a middle-aged lady and seemed pleasant enough.

I said, "Hello ma'am. I'm sorry, I live out of town. My cousin Porsche Winston lives here, and I was supposed to call her to pick me up from the airport, but I just took a taxi instead. I don't recall her apartment number. Could you be so kind to give it to me? I would love to surprise her." The lady initially looked apprehensive, but after I laid on the charm, I knew it wouldn't take much. I gave her just enough information to seem like I really knew her, and this old bitch sang like a canary. She even went on to say how sorry she was to hear she just lost her new husband. She went on and on about how sweet ole' girl was and how she seemed so happy with her new husband.

I had to politely cut her off. Old muthafucka's sure will tell all yo damn business without thinking twice. She gave me the apartment number and I flew to the elevator. I decided to take the elevators to the 13th floor and take the stairs the rest of the way. I didn't want to run into Marcus or the damn police. I got off the elevator and jetted up the stairs like I was in a relay. I cracked the stairwell and as luck would have it no one was in the hall. I eased down the call to apartment 1534. I could hear a lot of talking but could not decipher who it was.

I leaned closer to the door and out of nowhere some lady next door walked out of her apartment. She looked and said, "Gone knock baby. Someone in there." As much as I wanted to tell her to mind her own fucking business, I had to play it cool. I said, "Oh, you know I'm looking for apartment 1543, not

1534." I shook my head like I was truly lost. She said, oh baby, that's all the way down on the opposite side. You looking for Mr. Ron, right? He never gets visitors." I mustered up a smile and said, yeah, I guess today is his lucky day. I pretended to walk that way as she smiled and walked towards the elevators. Damn, does everyone know everybody in this fucking building? SHIT!

After the coast was clear I stood at the end of the hall just in time to see the detective step out of the door into the hall. I looked in rage as Marcus stepped outside the door and shook the man's hand like this was his bitch. That dude always gotta look so damn important. I can't wait to kill this muthafucka. I could hear the detective say, "We're definitely getting close. The partial print is being run through our database. We should get the results in 48 hours if all goes accordingly."

I heard Porsche tell the detective thank you as he walked to the elevator and they both turned to walk back into the apartment. The elevator doors closed, and I started pacing back and forth as everything was coming to fruition. I had to admit; my heart was pounding and for a moment, I felt like that scared kid in Juvey'. I shook off the nerves and said it's now or never. I knocked on the door and just as I thought, he answered...

*When It Comes Down To It*

# 31

## Porsche

On the way home, all I could think about was trying to find out what happened to Davarious. My mind would drift to different conversations and try to piece together any sort of hope that would lead to why someone would kill him. No matter how far in the left field my mind would go, it always came back to that Jay dude and how Davarious said he knew him and thought something was up with him. Suddenly, my mind drifted to Dee. I just can't believe she slept with that man. I mean a blind man can see he ain't on the up-and-up. I never would have thought she would have slept with anyone else, and especially a phony ass niggah like Jay. I knew she didn't have much experience with men, but damn. His ass has trouble written all over him. Uh, um, um, damn.

I didn't realize I said damn out loud, but the next thing I know Marcus was saying, "Porsche, it's going to be alright. They're going to get to the bottom of everything okay?"

All I could say was, "Yeah, I know. Thanks."

He had no clue I was thinking about his wife, my friend, miss gullible. All I could say is if this niggah had anything to do with Davarious' murder and he fucked over my friend? He's going to hate the day his momma didn't swallow his ass. We made it to the apartment and Marcus offered to see me in just to make sure I was okay. Marcus seemed like a pretty upstanding dude to me. I don't know why on earth Dee did what she did. Oh well, on the other hand, you never know what goes on behind closed doors so I'm going to try to stay out of Dee's mess. Hell, I've got my own shit to deal with.

I opened the door and Marcus had my bag and walked in. Just like a doting husband he called Dee to let her know we had arrived. After Marcus hung up the phone I said, "Hey, I appreciate everything you and Dee have done for me, but you don't have to stay. I'm cool, I'll just wait on Detective Wade to come."

Marcus looked at me like a father figure; "Girl, you know I'm not leaving you right now. Dee knows we're here. I'm going to stick around in case you need help with any of the questions. I'm just saying, just in case you need to get an attorney involved."

It dawned on me, that the first person of interest in a murder is the spouse! "Damn, Marcus, you're right. Good looking out. This muthafucka may try to go left on a Sista and I'm gonna have to kick his ass out then."

Marcus laughing, "Hold on Young Thug. Let's not jump to conclusions but just be on your Ps & Q's aight."

Marcus put my bag down and had a seat across the room near my bookshelf. I don't know why; everybody loves to sit in that damn chair. That's one thing I like about Marcus, he's old as a muthafucka, but he knows how to be respectful. Most dudes would have been trying to push up on a bitch even though I'm his wife's girl. I can say, he ain't never done no foul shit 'round me. I was standing in the kitchen wiping down the counter in the same damn spot when the doorbell rang. I looked at Marcus and he nodded as if he read my mind and knew I didn't have the courage to answer the door.

I just knew in my gut; it was detective Wade and as calm as I wanted to appear; I was about to jump out of my skin. My stomach was tied in knots, and I felt like I had the BG's! Before

Marcus opened the door I yelled, "Gone open the door, I'll be right back." Man, my stomach was turning flips, I couldn't handle this. I went to the restroom and sure enough, I had bubble guts. I got myself together and prayed no one heard me moaning like a sick cat in here. I washed up quickly and tried to fix up my frazzled hair. When I walked into the living room, Detective Wade was standing there like he was waiting for permission to sit down. I motioned for him to have a seat. Marcus sat across from him, and I sat in my high back gray chair facing the door.

Mr. Wade sat on the edge of the couch looking extremely "official." He said, "Mrs. Winston, again I am sorry for your loss and again we are working diligently to find answers to your husband's murder. Now, I know you stated you were home the night he was murdered. Can anyone vouch for you? It's not that I don't believe you, these are standard questions we ask."

Aww hell, I see where this is going. Good Marcus is here with me, I don't need this son of a bitch to try to mix my words and shit. I leaned forward in my chair and told him sternly; "I'll tell you like I told you when I reported him missing, I was home all night waiting for him to come home. If you check the phone records, you can see I called several times. As a matter of fact, can't y'all check the towers or some shit like that to see where I called from?" I was getting pissed from the mere fact this bastard tried questioning my story. I guess the detective could see this going wrong really quick. He softened his tone and assured me he believed me, but it was standard questioning. Marcus interjected and said, "Porsche, I believe you spoke with Dee a couple of times that night, didn't you?"

I did talk to Dee that night. Although I knew I had nothing to do with Davarious' death, the fact I spoke with Dee, and someone could confirm my story made a world of difference. I nodded confirming my conversation with Dee and turned my attention back to the detective. He asked a few more of the same damn questions as before. Like how long I had known him, did he talk about being in trouble, shit like that. Then he had the nerve to insinuate we got married fairly quick and asked did I feel I knew Davarious as well as I thought.

At that point, I couldn't hold it anymore. I went off! I asked "Who in the fuck do you think you are asking me some stupid shit like that? There's no timeframe on true love. Tha Fuck man!" I was going in, no holds barred. I kept hearing Marcus trying to tell me to calm down, but I wasn't trying to hear that bullshit. I mean, who did this dude think he was? Coming into my fucking house, asking me questions like he was trying to make me look guilty. I was so full of anger and grief, I looked at him and said, "You know what detective Wade, get the hell out! If you don't have any better leads for me, then don't bother me."

Detective Wade stood up and walked towards the door. "Mrs. Winston, again I apologize. I can imagine this is hard for you and in my line of work, I have to consider all avenues. I believe you had nothing to do with his murder, but we must ask all questions.

I said, "Detective, I get it. You're doing your job, but I lost the love of my life, and I don't know why. I can't eat, I can't sleep, I'm lost and on top of that, I feel like I'm being attacked, and you know what I do when I feel attacked? I come out muthafuckin' fighting like my life depends on it." I noticed he had a smirk on his face and tried to hide it, and truth be told I got tickled myself but this ain't no damn laughing matter.

He grabbed my hand and said, "Perhaps something sparked your memory. No matter how insignificant you may think it is, it could help so anything is important."

Right then, my mind went back to my conversations with Davarious about Jay. I looked at Marcus and timidly and said, "I don't know how significant this is, but Davarious did mention he thought he knew Marcus' business partner when we met that night at their house, but dude said Davarious was mistaken. I don't know if it's anything or not, but Davarious seemed to be certain he was someone else."

Marcus looked in disbelief as he lowered his eyes and asked, "Porsche, why didn't you say anything to me? I mean, he seems like a pretty stand-up dude."

I looked at Marcus like I wanted to stab his ass with a rusty butterknife. If he really knew what that niggah had been up to, he would be humming a different tune. "Stand up dude Marcus? Really? Man, get yo head out of the clouds. Shiittt, all you can see is the money he is bringing to the table." Fuck! Right then, I stopped and knew I had said too damn much! The detective looked at Marcus and Marcus stared at me with a look I had never seen before. To tell the truth, it shook me to my core. It was a cold, deadly look. I stood there scared as fuck, thinking I just messed things up for my girl. The detective said, Marcus, how well do you know this guy? Do you think he would have a reason to have a vendetta against Davarious?"

Marcus' kept staring at me like he was putting shit together in his head. Suddenly, he said "Naw man, I don't know. He's worked for me for about a year, but I don't know too much about his personals. I like my employees to keep their personal lives at home, so I don't ask about what they don't offer."

Marcus' tone, voice and demeanor all just changed in front of my eyes. He seemed more serious with a little swag and pinch of thuggishness to him. I wondered if Dee ever saw this side of him. I thought it was strange, but I dared not question. Detective Wade stood at the door as Marcus walked behind him. He turned to shake his hand and walked to the door. He turned around and said, "Mrs. Winston, trust the process. We're definitely getting close. The partial print is being run through our database. We should get the results in 48 hours if all goes accordingly."

I looked at him and said "Yeah, okay. I'll trust the process when you tell me you've caught the son-of-a-bitch who murdered Davarious but thank you." With that, he walked away. Marcus closed the door and I walked to the couch and fell back purely exasperated. I was expecting Marcus to quiz me about what I let slip out, but he didn't. Perhaps he knew I wasn't going to say any more than I already had. Maybe I was being paranoid, and he didn't catch what I said. Who am I fooling? He'd have to be the dumbest fucka on earth not to catch that innuendo and he's far from that.

He walked to the kitchen and asked if I needed anything before he left. I asked if he didn't mind grabbing me a drink and blunt from the white cookie jar on the kitchen counter. He looked at me and before he could say a word I said, "Look man, don't judge me, just hand me my shit. I don't do it often, but I need something to calm my nerves." He didn't say a word as he opened the jar and pulled out this fat blunt I had just for special occasions. He brought me the drink and as I lit up, I said, "And no, Dee does not smoke with me. As a matter of fact, she doesn't know about my little habit so let's keep it that way cool?"

Marcus laughed and said, "It's cool. Do you boo, no judgment from me. I'm going to give Dee a call and let her know I'm on the way. I'm sure she should be done with her conference call by now. You straight?"

As much as he wanted to appear like he wasn't thinking about what I said, we both could tell, he was calculating and putting some shit together in his head. Marcus called Dee and when she answered, it seemed like his apprehensions and curiosity disappeared and he was old Marcus again. She asked how I was, and he said, "Oh, she's just here having a drink and…trying to relax." I kept shaking my head because I just knew he was going to say something about my smoking. I yelled in the background thanking her for allowing Marcus to bring me home. They ended the call and Marcus got ready to leave. As soon as Marcus got ready to reach for the door, there was a knock. He looked at me and asked if I was expecting someone. I looked as surprised as he did because I don't have visitors. I initially thought the detective may have forgotten something. I told Marcus to go ahead and open the door and to my surprise, Jay's muthafuckin ass was standing there!

Marcus said, "Yo Jay man. Uhhh, what are you doing here?"

Before Jay could answer, I jumped off the couch and asked, "WHAT THE HELL'S GOING ON? HOW THE HELL DID YOU KNOW WHERE I LIVE AND WHAT THE FUCK DO YOU WANT?" As I was ranting and raving, his slick ass slid right by Marcus and had stepped inside the door. He said, "Hi Porsche, I know you don't know me well and this may seem a bit strange, but Marcus I just got an important call from Mr. Coi and there is a huge hiccup in the contract. I ran by your crib thinking you had returned, and Dee told me where to find you."

I screamed, "You fuckin Liar! We just spoke with Dee, and she would have mentioned if you came by…" All of a SUDDEN, I saw him reach out and Marcus doubled over in pain, went falling to the floor and I was standing there staring down the barrel of a pistol. This SON OF A BITCH stunned Marcus with a stun gun. Suddenly, he pulled out a large needle and stuck him in the neck. MARCUS WENT LIMP!! I screamed his name, and he didn't move. He never took his eyes off me as he kicked Marcus to the side like he was a piece of trash. As he held the gun, he walked closer to me and said "Sit tha Fuck Down Bitch!"

Needless to say, I sat my ass down. I couldn't help but keep looking at Marcus' lifeless body lying on the floor. I asked Jay, "What the hell's going on? What the fuck man?"

He walked toward me and pulled white zip ties from behind him. He looked like he was going to tie Marcus down first, but he thought better when he looked at me. It was like his ass knew if I got a second, I was going to give that muthafucka a run for his money, gun be damned! He said, "Oh you a bad bitch. Let's see how bad you are when yo ass is tied to this fucking chair." He grabbed my legs and zip-tied them so fast, I just knew this was not his first run with shit like this. He tied both my hands and proceeded to hog tie Marcus on the floor. He looked at me and said, "LET THE GAMES BEGIN!"

# 32

## Porsche

I sat in the chair pissed, scared, and fucking helpless. I wanted to scream, but I knew better. This crazy muthafucka meant business. And I knew at this point Jay killed Davarious! It had to be him. That was the only thing that made sense. The only question is why? I looked at Jay as he paced the floor. He walked back and forth around Marcus' lifeless body like a lion stalking its prey. I asked him, "Man, why are you doing this? What do you want?" He looked at me like I asked a rhetorical question.

He said, "What do I want? BITCH, WHAT DO I WANT? I'll tell you what I want. I want everything this muthafucka took from me and my family. That's what the fuck I want."

He had this look of disdain, anger and hurt all at the same time. I saw the hurt, but I couldn't feel any pity for this bastard. Hell, I was hurt, and I didn't understand what the hell was going on. I said, "Well if he took something from you what the fuck do I have to do with it? Why did you bring this shit to my house?" Just tell me, you killed Davarious didn't you? I know you did. Since you are so big and bad muthafucka, admit it. Then again, you're probably some little punk ass, limp dick having ass BIATCH! You wouldn't have had the balls enough to confront a man like Davarious!"

As soon as I said that Jay grabbed me around my neck and began to squeeze like he was trying to pop my damn head off my shoulders. One of his hands wrapped around my entire neck. My eyes began to water, not from fear or crying, but the mere pressure made me feel like my eyes were about to pop out of my head. He put his face close enough where I felt the warmth of his breath. He looked me directly in my eyes and with a calm, but dangerous voice said, "I will snap your neck with one fucking movement, bitch don't try me. Sit the fuck back and shut up before you end up joining your dearly departed."

He shoved my head against the back of the chair so hard until I felt like I had whiplash. I was sure I felt my brain splash against the back of my skull. A dirty bastard. He walked around the room as if he were trying to come up with a plan. As I sat there, I continued to contemplate what I could do to break free. My first thought was to jump him and run down the hall screaming for dear life. Common sense quickly made the change that train of thought.

I knew even if I were able to weasel out of these zip ties, there was no way I could overpower this big ass muthafucka. Besides if I did, he would surely shoot me in the back as soon as I made my way towards the door. Fuck, I would have to live on the 15th damn floor. Ain't no way my ass going to try to jump. Hmmm, but maybe I could find a way to push his ass out the window. Hell, I don't know, my head was spinning. All I know is I was in survivor mode, and I had to come up with something.

Jay sat on the barstool and turned where he could see the door, Marcus, and me all at the same time. He took a deep breath and leaned back as he helped himself to a glass of liquor. I tried to see some look of fear or discord, but he looked too damn calm.

I looked at him and said, "You're enjoying this shit, aren't you? Won't you just do what you're going to do and get it over with? Hell, I'm not afraid to die so fuck this, and fuck you."

He turned slowly and laughed. He said, "I must say, you are definitely a bold bitch. In any other situation, you probably could be a down ass chick. Yeah, go ahead and make peace with your God because you'll be meeting him soon if YOU DON'T SHUT THE FUCK UP!"

At that moment, a part of me felt he didn't want to kill me, but I figured I shouldn't continue to test the theory. Hell, if he did, he would have done it by now. Shit, I almost felt like Smokey in the movie Friday. I said, "I'll be quiet, but when you leave, I'll be talking again." I have no idea why I said that shit, but for a second, he let out a smirk and shook his head. As he turned around, he said, "crazy ass bitch."

Marcus started to moan and move a little on the floor. Jay turned around and said, "Oh, welcome to the party Marcus. I'm glad you could join us."

Marcus looked dazed and confused obviously still groggy from being drugged. He looked at Jay and said, "Man, what the fuck? You obviously don't know who you're fucking with."

Jay stood there with a grin on his face while staring down at Marcus like he wasn't shit. It almost seemed like he wanted to taunt Marcus like a child by saying NA, NAH, NA, NAH, NA. Marcus rolled on his side still confused and hog-tied.

Jay said, "Oh I know who I'm fucking with. The problem is you don't know who you're fucking with. But it's about time you learn. Yeah niggah, you gon' learn today! We just need a couple of people to join the party."

He turned to me and said, "Porsche, you're going to call Dee and Tammy and have them come over." Before I could object, Marcus yelled, "Bitch ass niggah, you leave my wife out of this!"

Jay looked surprised by Marcus' fearlessness. He said, "Ohhhh, you still talking shit and you're tied up like a hoe. I tell you what; when I need you, I'll yank your chain. In the meantime, GO TO SLEEP BITCH!"

As soon as Jay said that he made a running start and kicked Marcus on the left side of his face. Blood flew from his nose and mouth, and he was out cold. He calmly turned around and said, "now make the call or you're going to take a nap next, but yours may be a long dirt nap."

By this time, I was sick of his shenanigans. I had nothing to lose so I was not going to bite my tongue. I said, "Fool, I can't call anyone if my hands are tied. To be so smart, you one dumb muthafucka." As soon as I said that I regretted it because he slapped the shit out of me. Hell, I pissed myself a little. Damn, I've never been slapped before. How the hell do women deal with that shit from abusive men? Hell naw, I can't.

He grabbed my phone and held it to my face to unlock it. By this time, I was tearful and exasperated. He said, "Call Dee and tell her Marcus left his phone and you need her because you thought you could be alone, but you can't."

I looked at him with so much hatred. If looks could kill, he would be one dead fucka. He scrolled through my contact until he came to her name. As he pressed send and held the phone to my mouth, I felt this lump in my throat. I was so messed up, I thought I would vomit right then and there. Dee answered the phone and with my voice trembling, I said exactly what he wanted. I'm sure she assumed I was still crying over Davarious so my weak voice would not be a giveaway for her. Dee agreed but initially said she would wait until Marcus arrived home. I came up with the lie that he said he was stopping by his office, and I really needed her to come right away. She agreed and said she would be here in 20 minutes. I felt sick to my stomach knowing that my friend is going to walk into some real shit she ain't about to be ready to handle.

Jay ended the call and said, "You did well. All y'all bitches can lie at the drop of a hat. I just may spare you after all. Now call the THOT Tammy."

I said, "Look, Tammy ain't ever been to my house. It's going to be really strange me calling her out of the blue to come over here."

He shook his head apprehensively, "Oh, I see the bar and I smell weed in here. It ain't going to be hard for you to get her to come over.

He scrolled through my contacts and found Tammy's name. I wanted to ask what Tammy had to do with all of this, but I didn't feel like getting slapped again so I just did what I was told.

The phone rang several times, and the voicemail came on. Her voicemail had one of the most ratchet messages in the world. I don't know why people have stupid ass messages on their phones. And she wonders why no one ever took her seriously. A damn shame. The voicemail said, *"You've reached the Bitch you love to hate. If I don't fuck with chu, don't bother leaving a message. Now do what you do.*" I said, "Tammy, this is Porsche, give me a call when you get this message. I moved my head away from the phone and Jay ended the call. I looked at Jay and said, "no answer man; the voicemail came on."

Jay looked at me like I was stupid and said, "No shit Sherlock! Now call her back and keep calling until the bitch answers the fucking phone!"

I prayed she wouldn't answer. I really didn't want to get her involved with this and I don't know what he had up his sleeve for her. He waited a moment and called again. He pushed the phone against my face so hard like he was trying to break my jaw.

This time Tammy answered, "Bitch what's so damn important and why are you calling me like you my niggah or something?"

I sat there for a second to collect myself because I didn't know how I was going to get this girl to come over here. I mean we deal with each other, but not well enough to be coming over. I tried to play it cool. "Hey Tammy, it's been a minute."

Tammy said, "Hell yeah, it's been a minute. Ohhhh, girl I heard about yo man. Bitch, I'm so sorry about that shit. That's fucked-to-the–up. You gone be aight."

As ghetto as she sounded, I knew that was about the best kind of sympathy I was going to get from her. I don't think we really talked since Davarious and I got serious. Maybe a few times, but not enough for me to be calling her for consolation.

I tried to hold it together and said, "Yeah, I'ma be alright. Tammy, I'm sitting here on that brown and loud. I was thinking if you ain't tied up, you could stop by and light up a few with me." As soon as I said that I got this huge lump in my throat. I felt like a sell-out for allowing this bastard to coax me into calling both Dee and Tammy.

Tammy started laughing, "Ohhh, you decide to call a down ass bitch cuz Ms. Prissy must be out of town being bougie or something. Then again, she's prolly too goodie-two-shoes to smoke. Well, I ain't got too much going on today. I'll roll up."

Before she could finish, I rushed to give her my address. "Tammy, you know I still live in Midtown Park, apartment 1534. I'll call downstairs and let the receptionist know I'm expecting you."

"Umm, call down to tell the receptionist? Y'all know y'all some straight bougie ass hoes. I'll see you in a lil bit."

Tammy ended the call and I looked up at Jay. He had a look of satisfaction as he sat on the arm of the chair.

# 33

# Dee

I sure hope Marcus is okay. He left his phone. Well, he can be forgetful, but I don't know how, especially since all he's done lately is hold on to his phone and answer every call making sure all is well with that deal in Japan.

I knew Porsche wasn't ready to be alone. Hell, if something like this happened to Marcus, I don't know what I would do. I would be a basket case! As I jumped in my new black 2016 Tesla and headed to Porsche's apartment, I figured I would stop and bring her something to eat. I dialed her number; it rang a few times and went to voicemail. I tried to call Marcus' phone just in case she happened to look at it and see it was me calling. Hmmmm, that's strange, it went to voicemail too. I waited a couple of moments and called back. Porsche answered.

I said, "Girl, what are you doing? I called your phone and Marcus. I was checking to see what you wanted to eat. I know you don't have any groceries and you need to keep something in your stomach."

Porsche in a meek, almost desperate voice said, "Uhhh, yeah I went to the bathroom. You know I wasn't going to answer Marcus' phone. Besides Dee, I can't eat right now. Bring whatever you feel like bringing and I may nibble on something."

I said, "Ooookayyyy then, I'll bring you something light. You know you gotta eat. You can't make yourself physically sick." Porsche mumbled "ummhmm, okay Dee," and hung up.

I looked at the phone to double-check that the call ended. I've got to get my friend through this.

# 34

## Tammy

For as long as I've known Porsche, she ain't never invited me to her place. We kick it, but we would always meet for lunch or a girls' night out. She must be in a really bad place to call me. I mean I feel bad for her in all, but shit, she acts like they were married for ten years and he died. I could see some real grieving over that, but hell the paint ain't dried on the walls of their relationship and she's acting like she's going to dig a grave and join the muthafucka. Shhhhhiiitt, I guess a bitch like me ain't built like that. Men come a dime a dozen. Hmph, I would shed a tear over his ass in the morning, cash the insurance check that afternoon, and be riding another dick that night. I've never met one worth the funk in an asshole, so I say fuck'em. Fuck all of 'em.

Porsche wants to smoke something but she prolly got some weak ass "Reggie" so I'm going to bring my own shit. I'll grab some of that Kush or Loud. If a bitch plan to get high, I wanna be in the clouds. She usually keeps it simple when it comes to drinking, but I have seen her order some high-dollar shit when we kick it. I'm going to bring some Crown just in case she is having one of those bougie days. Hell, I'm a plain muthafucka; give me my Crown and Coke and I'm Gucci.

I made sure I locked up my shit and hopped in my black 2011 Toyota Camry. Yeah, that bitch is about 5 years old, but she's clean as a muthafucka. Tinted with the black RTX Black Widow Satin rims! And that engine purrs like a kitten; she's on point.

I decided not to take the expressway and chose the scenic route. I have to get my mind right to kick it with females. As cool as Porsche is, females be moody as hell, especially when they got shit going on in their life. (Tammy laughing to herself) Hmph, as cold as I am; I should have been a damn dude!

I decided to light up as I cruised to 21 Savage's "No Heart." I heard that joint when I was kicking it with this dude from ATL and he was playing' the shit. I told him that was me all day long, No damn Heart!

I finally rolled up to the address Porsche gave me. I must admit, it's a pretty nice part of town. I cruised towards the front doors as my music vibrated through my soul. I slowed and rolled my window down just to make sure I was at the right place. Some old lady walking in gave me a look like she was trying to scold me for having my music turned up. I turned it down and yelled, "Aunt Bea, get yo old ass in there. Ain't, you heard music before?" She turned around so fast that she almost stumbled into the door. I said to myself, "that's what I thought."

A doorman walked up and asked if he could help me or if I needed valet parking. I told him, "Man, hell to the no. I don't need valet parking; I can park my own shit. I ain't giving you my keys to rifle through my stuff." He looked at me and said, "Ma'am, are you sure you're at the right place?" I was getting ready to cuss his ass completely out but I decided not to. Hell, I'm in this prissy ass side of town and high as fuck. I don't need to go to anybody's jail. I just gave him the deadliest look I could and spun off. I rolled to the side of the building and saw a good spot. I backed in like an OG and rolled up my windows. I lit up one more time to get a final hit before I go in here and try to be sympathetic.

As I walked to the building, I couldn't help but feel a little envy. I mean, I've done well for myself, but none of these bitches could have lived like I lived and survived. They had shit handed to them. I've had to scratch and scrape my way to the top. I mean just look around, doormen and shit, valet parking… These hoes don't have a clue. The only doorman I've had was the crackhead I kicked out of the way because he passed out in front of the door.

As I walked through the entrance; I tugged at my canary yellow skirt. It kept riding up these thick thighs the tricks be drooling over. My ass may not have much weight on it, but I make up for it with these thighs that can crush a watermelon. I stopped at the receptionist desk and asked for Porsche Davis' apartment. This old ass decrepit looking bitch looked at me like I stole something. I stood back on one leg and put my hand on my hips and said, "You couldn't have heard me because you are standing here looking lost. I SAID POINT ME TO THE ELEVATORS TO PORSCHE DAVIS' APARTMENT, DAMN!"

She gleamed at me like an usher in church and replied; "I heard what you said young lady. Is she expecting you? She sure has had a few visitors today. It's so unlike Ms. Porsche. I guess giving the circumstances…"

Before she could finish, I cut her off. You can tell she's one nosey heifer. I said, "I wouldn't be here if she weren't. Look lady…" Just as I was about to break her down like a fraction, I heard a sound like an elevator from around the corner. I decided she wasn't worth my time and waved her off. I said, "Just in time, I see where I need to go, thanks for nothing." I dashed on the elevator as some preppy-looking dude got off. Thank goodness I was on the elevator alone. I didn't feel like anyone trying to have small talk and shit. Shhhhitttt, I got to fuck with Porsche's ass for me to come to this side of town.

Before I knew it, doors opened. I was standing there looking at the sign on the wall to determine if I needed to go left or right. I turned left and looked down this long corridor hallway. The walls were a light almond color with darker circular designs in the paint. There was a hint of burgundy and navy blue here and there and it seemed to give the walls a bit of a pop. I never would have put those colors together, but it was working. There were expensive looking paintings on the walls and decorative lights above each door. A few doors down the hall, there were apartments across from one another. The doors were much wider than the others so I assumed those may have been Penthouses. I looked at the numbers on the right side of the door and wouldn't you know it; This bitch lives in a penthouse! No wonder why she didn't want anyone to visit. Always trying to downplay shit like she has to work for hers. All the while, this hoe living large off daddy's money. I can't hate on her though. She always comes off as down to earth. You wouldn't peg her for the rich type. Not like her prissy ass homegirl.

I gave my skirt one more tug before I knocked on the door. I stood there for what seemed like forever. I know this bitch didn't call me over here and her ass ain't answering the damn door. What the Fuck Man! I turned to walk towards the elevators. Before I stepped away, I could hear Porsche in a weak ass voice yell, "Just a minute."

I mean, she asked a bitch to come over, then her ass ain't ready. I stood there shaking my leg like I was about to piss on myself. For one, I was hell. I had been drinking on that damn YAK and smoking, I really had to piss. I yelled through the door; "Bitch hurry yo ass up! You knew my ass was coming over, Come on hell."

It sounded like there was some mumbling behind the door and then I heard Porsche say "IIIIItttt's open!"

I walked through the door and noticed the décor. Porsche was sitting in a high back gray chair facing the door. She looked like she had been in a fight, and she didn't have the upper hand. I said' "Damn Bitch, what's up? You know I almost set out 'bout three or four folks before I even got on the damn elevator. It's some nosey ass people 'round here. You ain't tell me you lived in such a bougie-ass neighborhood. Bitch if you weren't my girl. Anyway, where the drinks at?" I walked towards the bar to help myself to a drink. No use putting off what I came to do. I turned left to step into the kitchen and was caught off guard. He was standing in the kitchen with this wild-ass look on his face. Porsche, what is this muthafucka doing here? You didn't tell me anyone else was going to be here. I hope you ain't trying to play no matchmaker shit. I don't play dem kind of games. Before even giving Porsche the opportunity to answer, I turned to him. "And since when did y'all know each other, where y'all kicking it? I knew there was something foul about this niggah, but Porsche, I ain't know you were on some hoe shit."

In all my talking, I noticed Porsche hadn't said a word. Suddenly, I realized the disheveled look as a look of fear and not exhaustion. He leaned over towering me as I looked up at him like a child would look up at her mother. He said, "So glad you decided to join the party."

"Party, What damn party? Porsche, what kind of fucked up shit you got going on?" I glanced down and noticed a body lying on the floor at the opposite end of the bar. I turned to run towards the door but he grabbed me by my hair and dragged me back like I was a rag doll. Out of all days, my ass didn't have a wig on. If I had a wig, he could have snatched that shit and I would have been out this bitch! Fuck! He slung me down to the floor. My dress rolled halfway up my ass. I didn't give a fuck though; a bitch was on survival mode.

This scenario seemed all too familiar. A trick slapping my ass around… Hell naw, I gotta get out of this shit. I crawled towards the body, and he grabbed the back of my head again. I heard Porsche screaming "Stop, stop, what did we ever do to you?" I guess I got some strength from somewhere because I felt like I was dragging that muthafucka on my back. As soon as I made it close enough to see the person lying there, I yelled; "Xander!" and then all went black…

# 35

## Jay

Jay stood over Marcus and Tammy after zip-tying and gagging them both. With a look of pride and accomplishment, he thought; *"Let me make sure I tie these muthafucka's good. My, my, my... Look at badass Marcus Alexander or shall I say the infamous Xander and his thirsty sidekick Tammy!"* Porsche looked confused as Jay walked around Marcus and Tammy's lifeless bodies like a lion stalking his prey. Jay noticed Porsche's dismay and asked; "Oh, don't worry, they ain't dead! At least not yet. It'll wear off soon enough and if not, I've got something that will wake their ass fast. I refuse to let them die this easy."

Porsche looked as if she contemplated asking questions or if she should continue to try to figure out this puzzle on her own. Against her better judgment she asked, "Why are you doing this, and who is Xander? You called Tammy his sidekick? Man, fuck, you've got me tied to this damn chair and they are lying there half dead. Shit, I told you I ain't scared no more. The least you could do is tell me what the hell this got to do with me and Davarious!!!!"

Jay looked up and walked towards Porsche. "You still don't get it, do you? But you will and you will as soon as that hoe of a friend gets here."

Jay looked at the door and anger arose like lava exploding from a volcano; "*WHERE IS THAT BITCH? DID YOU TIP HER OFF? I AIN'T GOT ALL DAMN DAY!!!*"

Porsche raised her voice although trembling with fear, "I CALLED HER, WHAT ELSE DO YOU WANT ME TO DO?? I TELL YOU WHAT, JUST KILL ME NOW AND GET THIS SHIT OVER WITH!"

Jay laughed like he was at a comedy show. Just then, the doorbell rang. The laughing stopped and he motioned for Porsche. Realizing she was still tied to the chair, he ran over and slit the ties off of her wrists. He snatched Porsche out of the chair and pushed her towards the door. Porsche looked back at him as if this was her last plea to stop. She slowly turned the knob and stood there guarding the door like she was trying to prevent Dee from entering. Jay stood on her right while he nudged her with the gun. Porsche glared at Dee hoping she could read her mind as if she were trying to plead with her to turn around and leave now! Dee never picked up on the hint and walked through the door. Unbeknownst to her, things would change forever.

# 36

## Dee

"Hey girl. You are standing there like you're scared to let me in or something. What's up?" I was smiling expecting one of Porsche's snide remarks. My smile faded because I was caught off guard when I walked in to see Jay's face. I looked at Porsche with confusion. Porsche stood there frozen, afraid to move. Suddenly I noticed Jay holding a gun at Porsche's side as he coaxed her back to her chair while demanding I have a seat. Porsche cried out, "Dee, I'm sorry, I'm so sorry. He made me, he made me... call y'all."

Jay pushed her back in the chair and tied her hands together so fast even Porsche was surprised she was yet again confined to the chair.

I was still baffled but I asked; "Call y'all? Call who? Porsche what is he doing here; what's going on?"

As soon as I said that I glanced over and saw Marcus and Tammy lying on the floor! I dropped the bags of take-out and screamed.

"What have you done? Marcus! Marcus!" I saw Tammy but at that moment I had tunnel vision and ran right past Tammy straight to Marcus. I could see he was breathing and seemed to be arousable but couldn't quite keep open his eyes. I attempted to pull the gag out of his mouth. Jay grabbed my hand away from his mouth but allowed me to lie there with him. He said, "Uh, Uh, uh, not so fast baby. You leave that towel right there. If his punk ass makes a wrong move; his shit is over."

I looked at Jay and said, "You would go to this length to have me? What the hell's wrong with you? I told you I loved Marcus. What have you done?" I laid on Marcus' side and sobbed uncontrollably but my tears were short-lived as Jay began to laugh hysterically.

Jay said, "Bitch, you really still think this is about you? It's never been about you. This is all about Xander and what he took from me.

At that point, I was even more puzzled. I looked over at Porsche, then back to Jay. "Xander? Who is Xander?"

Jay was frustrated with my ignorance. He exhaled like I was supposed to be able to read his mind or something. He said, "Bitch, you still don't know who Xander is??? All that damn college degree and you are too stupid to put two and two together? Your last name is Alexander, right? Xander, short for Alexander? The infamous King-Pin Xander?"

I sat there clueless. This obviously had to be a mistake. Marcus was never called Xander, and he certainly was never involved with drugs.

Suddenly Jay said, "I see I have to break it down for your ass. All that damn book smarts and you as flakey as a buttermilk biscuit. Get up!"

I slowly got off the floor and tried to run towards Porsche's side. Jay reached out to stop me and I tripped and fell face first on the marble floor. I don't know if he pushed me or if I fell on my own, but he laughed with satisfaction. As I laid there bleeding, I heard Porsche yell; "You dirty bastard! Now yo ass just being petty. Don't no real man do no shit like that. That was a real bitch move."

As blood continued to spill from my nose, Jay sat me up on the floor. For a brief moment, I thought he was going to help me, but all he did was tied my hands behind me and my feet to the leg of Porsche's table.

Jay walked around like he had won a medal. He said, "now we're going to deal with the real."

He walked to Marcus and pulled out something and put it under his nose. Marcus immediately woke up! He was yelling something, but it was difficult to ascertain what he was saying with the gag in his mouth. I could tell by his face, whatever he was saying; there were some serious threats involved. Jay's strong muscular build came in handy because he grabbed Marcus like he was lightweight and sat him up on the floor. He looked over and pulled a chair from the table. He sat the gun on the back of the couch and reached to help Marcus off the floor to the chair. He stood behind Marcus and yelled, "Get up sorry ass Niggah."

Marcus stood loosely and obviously groggy from whatever Jay had done. Jay pushed him in the chair and grabbed some rope from his jacket pocket. He tied Marcus tightly to the chair. Marcus sat slumped in the chair still fighting to overcome whatever he had been given. I kept glancing at the gun on the chair knowing I had no chance of getting loose or overpowering him at all. At this point, Porsche seemed more angry than scared. Suddenly, I looked over and remembered Tammy was lying on the floor. Truth be told, I forgot all about her when I saw Marcus. I've never been a fan, but I wouldn't dare want her hurt or tied up in my triangle. I kept sitting there still oblivious to the reason why he chose to do this. All I could think was he was a deranged lover scorned and he wanted to ruin my life.

Jay turned around looking for the gun and spotted it on the chair. He noticed me staring and said, "Bitch, whatever you're thinking, keep it in that pretty little head of yours. Don't try me because neither you nor your sorry ass husband knows who the fuck I am." He stood next to Marcus and pushed against his head with the gun and said, "Ain't that right, Xander!"

I said, "who the hell is Xander? Why do you keep calling him that? Marcus, what's going on?"

Jay looked at me in disbelief and scratched his head with the barrel of his gun. I was hoping it would go off and blow his freaking head off.

Jay said, "well now the gang's all here. At least everyone who needs to be, I can enlighten you my dear. See Marcus ain't who you think he is baby girl. And Xander, I mean Marcus, your precious Dee ain't who you think she is. As a matter of fact, WHEN IT COMES DOWN TO IT; all y'all muthafuckas got some crosses to bear." He looked at Porsche who sat there quietly and said, "even you P."

Porsche screamed; "LOOK I DON'T EVEN KNOW YOU. DEE THIS MAN KILLED DAVARIOUS, I KNOW HE DID!"

Jay's eyes pierced her soul and totally ignoring her comment about Davarious said; "BLAH, BLAH, BLAH. No, you don't know me, but you know someone who was once close to me and if it weren't for you, THEY WOULD STILL BE HERE!"

Porsche was even more confused than I was. Jay went on ranting and raving about his life and what was taken, but yet never said anything that made sense to us. He paced back and forth from Porsche and me to Marcus and Tammy who had not moved. I wondered if she was dead. Part of me felt guilty because I thought she was innocent in all this. I kept wondering how my selfishness got us into this situation. If I only hadn't slept with him, if I told Marcus when he first came by the house or even if I weren't as friendly at the bar; none of this would have happened... Suddenly, Porsche's phone rang. Jay stopped ranting and grabbed the phone from the table. In a panic, he pushed the phone to Porsche's face and told her to answer and not to say anything out of the way. He turned to Marcus and me and said, "Don't make a fuckin' sound." Marcus was still slumped in the chair in and out of consciousness.

Porsche cleared her throat; "Hello. Yes, this is she. Yes, I have a moment." Jay grabbed the phone and put it on speaker. He muted the line for a second and said, "don't try to be superwoman bitch, you got it!"

He unmuted the phone and laid it on Porsche's lap on speaker. You could hear a man's voice saying "Hello, Hello Mrs. Winston, are you there?"

Porsche cleared her voice again, "Yes, I'm sorry detective Wade, I'm here."

"Great Mrs. Winston. I was calling to let you know we have a major break in the case. We have a match to the partial print. Does the name Tylea Jackson ring a bell?"

Porsche looked like she had seen a ghost. She held the phone and suddenly she unconfidently said; "Ummmm, no, no; the name doesn't ring a bell. Who is it?" Porsche held her head down as tears began to fall. She obviously knew who this Tylea person was. You could tell she was hiding something.

Mrs. Winston. Tylea Jackson was a petty criminal back in the day. A couple of prostitution charges and later a distribution with the intent to sell. For some reasons, people thought she was dead. Perhaps she resurfaced and this was a robbery gone wrong. I'm so sorry again. Are you sure the name doesn't ring a bell?"

As tears continued to fall, she exclaimed; "I said I didn't know her, didn't I? Did you catch her?"

"No, we haven't, but we will be looking."

"Well detective, until you do; don't call me. Now if you don't mind, I have to go." Porsche hung her head again as Jay hung up the phone. She began to sob uncontrollably. She said, "How could he? Did I drive him to do this? Is Davarious' death my fault?"

Jay looked at her with discontent. "You think? Of course, it's your fault. That's what y'all bitches do. Pretend like you've got a niggah's back and when shit gets real, you rush to the next dick in line. Ain't none of y'all shit!"

Porsche kept her head down and raised her guilt-ridden eyes. "You don't know shit about me. I don't know if your mammy didn't give you enough hugs or if she left you on the nip too fuckin long, but you got some fucked up shit going on.

Niggah, I'm sick of this. Either you do what you came to do, or you get the fuck out."

Jay turned around calmly and said, "Okay then." SUDDENLY I HEARD SOMETHING THAT ZIPPED PAST ME!!!! I screamed when I looked over and saw Porsche doubled over in pain.

I yelled, "WHAT DID YOU DO? WHAT HAVE YOU DONE?" I pulled against the ties and kicked the legs of the table I was tied to like my life depended on it. Hell, my life did depend on it and if I was going to help Porsche, I needed to do something drastic.

I saw blood pour from Porsche's leg. This bastard shot Porsche! And didn't even blink!

Jay looked at Porsche and said, "See, now look what you made me do? You were going to be my ride or die, but your ass talks too damn much. So now, you sit here and babysit that little bullet wound of yours. Trust, you'll be aight."

Porsche mustered up some strength from somewhere. She asked; "Can you at least give me something to wrap my leg?"

He looked over at me like he was contemplating something. He walked over and cut the ties and said, "go get a towel or something and tie her leg so her ass won't bleed every damn where. I sat for a moment in disbelief. I couldn't believe part of him trusted me or it could have been he knew I didn't have the courage enough to do anything other than what was asked. Or so he thought…

I ran towards Porsche's bedroom. Jay yelled; "Now you know damn well, I ain't letting yo slick ass out of my sight. Go in the damn kitchen and get a towel and keep your ass where I can see you."

I looked around the kitchen grabbed a couple of towels from the drawer. As I turned to step back into the living room, I thought about the roll of tape Porsche keeps in what she calls her junk drawer under the counter. Suddenly Jay yelled; "GET YO ASS IN HERE NOW!"

I almost skipped the step trying to get back to Porsche. I ran to her side and pressed the towels around her wound. I took the gray tape and started wrapping like a madwoman. Porsche screamed; "Damn Dee! This ain't no muthafuckin papercut, shit!"

Porsche continued to cry off and on. I didn't know if it was from the gunshot, Davarious' death, or if there was more to that call from the detective than she let on. She never mentioned knowing a Tylea Jackson to me, but it seemed like she was hiding something.

I sat beside Porsche nursing her leg. Jay didn't seem to be worried about me. I could hear Marcus moan in and out of consciousness, but oddly enough, I never heard a peep out of Tammy. Part of me wondered if she was dead, but I dared not ask.

Marcus began to moan louder, and Jay walked over. He said, "about time sleeping beauty. I know you didn't think I wasn't going to wait on you. Hell, you're the guest of honor."

He turned and looked at me and said, "You still don't get it do you Boo Boo. Well, the chickens have come home to roost. As my old ass probation officer use to say."

I looked even more confused and thought to myself; "Probation Officer? What the hell?" I guess he could tell I had so many questions and suddenly he because angrier and turned to Marcus.

Jay snatched the gag from Marcus' mouth and said, "Niggah ain't you tired of this? Gone tell yo bitch who you are and why we are ALL HERE!"

Marcus yelled; "Mane, I don't know you what the fuck you are talking about. All I know is you really don't know who you're dealing with…"

Jay cut him off, "I know, and you know that I know (looking down at Tammy laying on the floor) and that bitch knows. Yo shit is ova." He turned to me and yanked off the floor. He said, "Seems like we all got secrets and now is the time to come clean."

"Yo Xander, did you know I've been fuckin' your bitch for months? Didn't know that huh? So damn slick, and yo bitch was screwing me right under your nose." He looked at me with the most cunning smile and said, "ain't that right baby?"

I started to sob and pleaded with Marcus, "baby, he made me, he said he would ruin us, he said…"

Marcus had a fiery look that I had never seen before; "Dee, what the fuck you mean made you? Are you telling me you've been fuckin this niggah? And if he made you, why the hell didn't you say something to me; I could have…? This niggah been all in our house? What, so you a skank ass hoe now? When, where how did this start?"

Jay interjected; "Ummm, let me answer that for you, my man. The first of many times; right in that little nest egg of y'alls. She was especially ready the night of your party. You slept like a baby."

Marcus jumped towards us like he was going to kill someone. The question was who; me or Jay. Marcus suddenly sat back in his chair with a calm demeanor like he was taking it all in. Jay said, "Xander my man don't blame her, she was just the average young, sex, adventure starved wife married to an old ass, predictable niggah. It was easy as taking candy from a baby. Besides, it ain't about her at all. This is all on you and what you did to me."

I stood there like a child being scolded by her parent too afraid to look at Marcus. With my head held down I said, "Marcus, I, I'm sorry. He…"

Marcus lowered his eyes almost like he felt sorry for me and let out a loud sigh; "Dee, don't okay. I'll deal with you later."

Jay snidely said; "Aww, he still loves you even after knowing you ain't no different than the rest of these bitches. Money, attention, and power are what you all want. You are always ready for the highest bidder."

Suddenly Jay pushed me to the floor. Marcus lunged forward only to fall over in the chair. He was obviously still feeling the effects of whatever Jay gave him. Marcus looked at me then back at Jay. He said, "You better kill me. If you don't, call whatever piece of family you have and tell them to plan your funeral because there's going to be some slow singing and flower bringing for yo ass."

Jay angrily spewed; "FAMILY? FAMILY MY NIGGAH?" He stared at Marcus while turning his attention to me. Dee, let me introduce you to the infamous Xander Alexander. The man who single-handedly destroyed me and my sister's life. See baby girl, your dude use to be the biggest Kingpin around. He had people running dope all across this country. But! Prior to that, his ass was a pimp. And not just a Pimp, THE PIMP! He had niggahs and bitches scared to think of his name. Of course, you wouldn't know any of that because like any pedophile ass niggah, he found someone much younger who was too young to know shit about his ass.

I looked at Marcus and tearfully asked; "Babe, what is he talking about?"

Jay ignored my question to Marcus and said, "Like I said when it comes down to it; everyone has secrets."

# 37

## Marcus

I knew at some point in my life, my past would come to hunt me. I just didn't know it would be like this. I cannot believe Dee disrespected our home. If I were who I use to be, I wouldn't have given two fucks what she did. I sat in the chair tied drifting in and out of consciousness. I thought about all the shit I've done in my life and wondered how this dude fits into the equation. I ordered hits and did so much foul shit, I would never be able to drill down who or why this man felt the need to infiltrate my life. He had to have studied my life for quite some time. There were three old heads who got out of the game when I did.

I paid them to be security over the years because I never knew when or if someone would be bold enough to try to come for me. After a few years, things were pretty quiet and getting to what I thought was normal. One of my soldiers ended up getting back in the life and sad to say, was murdered. I found out while watching the news one evening. The life as we knew it was all he ever knew so staying out of the game proved to be harder for him than anticipated.

The last two dudes served me well and stuck to the agreement of staying out of the game, away from the extracurriculars and watching my back. About a year ago we agreed it had been long enough and security was no longer needed. Besides, they needed a life. They dedicated their lives to making sure no one tried to knock me off or my new unsuspecting wife. I guess it was about that time that ole boy showed up.

I was angry at Dee, but I mostly felt this was my fault. Women like Dee don't peep games like the average Thirst Bucket. Besides, I let my guard down, this is all on me.

I sat tied to the chair feeling less than the man I knew I was. The more time in this chair, the more time I had to reflect on shit I overlooked with this niggah. For one, no family and how he was never too far away. I realized at that moment, I relied heavily on my guys to keep watch of every part of my life. With them gone, I left an opening for this muthafucka to slither in.

I felt it was time to confirm what Jay told Dee about me. I've never lied about who I was; I omitted unnecessary shit that wasn't relevant to who I am now.

"Dee, look. I used to be called Xander years ago. I did a lot of things I am not proud of, however, I'm no longer that man. I worked hard to change my life and I made you the woman who I would spend the rest of my life with. That's what it is and all you need to know is I loved you and I am not who he thinks I am."

*Jay became furious with Marcus' blasé explanation.* "Is that what you call coming clean? Is that what you call the truth? Man, you've spent your entire life cheating, killing, destroying others and you have convinced yourself that it was nothing! I tell you what! Let's see how nonchalant yo ass is when I knock you off!"

Jay feverishly started to pace back and forth. All the while he told the story of how I ruined his life. He went on and on about me, Tammy, and his only family. I've done so much shit, I had not one clue of what family he was talking about. Hell, especially since he said Tammy. She was my main bottom bitch, so heaven only knows who we crossed. Suddenly, the rants stopped, and he squatted down to look into my eyes. It was strange, especially since no man had ever had the nerves to look towards my face, never-the-less stare in my eyes. Jay said, "Xander, maybe this will jog your memory."

*Szzzippppp!*

He shot me in the arm! The silencer muffled the loud noise where all you heard was a faint sound. I had never been shot before. The bullet sizzled through my arm like a branding iron. It burned like hell, but it was tolerable. Dee screamed. He hit Dee in the mouth to quieten her and turned to see Porsche lying to the side and Tammy still motionless on the floor.

Jay said, "Dee, shut the fuck up! The fucking police is going to be here in a moment with all that damn yelling. Xander, I'm sure you remember the California run that I heard fucked you out of millions. Well, Tammy's girl, the woman you thought you killed, lived and so did her brother you paid to have beaten on the regular in jail to ensure silence now stands before you. Not as the scared little boy, but the man who is going to watch you suffer. You fucked up my life! You destroyed my sister! So much so until she wanted to be a man. And let's not forget TAMMY!" SZZzippppp.

He shot towards Tammy on the floor, but she never moved. The bullet sounded as if it ricocheted off the floor and hit the cabinet. He looked at Porsche lying helpless in the chair and said "Yeah, my sister became a man, and You KNOW WHAT PORSCHE, THE one time he was brave enough to love, YOU LEFT HIM! That's right you left Tye and so HE MOVED AND left the only family he had… ME!"

Porsche's eyes became as huge as headlights. She said, "You're, you're Tye's brother? But you don't understand… Is this why he killed Davarious?

Jay said, "Ooh I understand. YOU ALL are sooo tied up thinking you're perfect and your secrets won't come out, but I studied y'all. I watched night and day. I'm so glad I blackmailed that guard to switch our fingerprints back in the day. I knew it would come in handy. Y'all fucked us, now we fucking you!!!"

Jay thought back to Porsche's last question. "Don't you get it Porsche, I killed Davarious; Tye would never have the nerve to do that! He was getting in my business, so I had to make sure he stayed quiet!"

Dee raised her head towards Porsche and asked; "So you did know who the detective asked about. Porsche, is this why you and Tye broke up? You could have told me; I would have understood."

Jay stammered, "You know what Bitch, you don't understand shit!"

*SZIPPPPPP, SZIPPPPPP*

Dee fell limp on the floor. A pool of blood started to flow from behind her back and head. I yelled in despair. "I'll kill you!"

Jay turned and walked close to me and pressed the gun against my head. Suddenly Porsche leaped and jumped on Jay's back! She was crying and fighting like a madwoman. Jay was flinging her from side to side as she stuck to him with her arms wrapped tightly around his neck. Jay tried to aim the gun up to shoot behind him; all to no avail. Porsche was holding for dear life.

All Of a Sudden, Jay grabbed Porsche by the arms and flipped her to the floor. He stood over her with satisfaction and got ready to pull the trigger.

*THE DOOR FLEW OPEN.*

Detective Wade with four other officers ran in. He yelled; "Freeze! DON'T DO IT! Put the gun down JayShawn Jackson Crawford!"

Jay looked surprised that detective Wade knew his old and alias name. He dropped the gun and fell to his knees angry that he didn't finish the job. One of the rookies ran over and cuffed him, while another called the paramedics.

Detective Wade said Jay Crawford aka JaShawn Jackson has been wanted in Rhode Island for racketeering for some time now. Once I crossed referenced the partial print found at the scene; I searched for any relatives of Tylea Jackson and as luck would have it; JaShawn Jackson showed up. He looked at Porsche and said; "You're one brave lady Mrs. Winston. How were you able to text me?"

Porsche looked at Dee's lifeless body and said; "Dee. Dee gave me cuticle scissors she grabbed from the drawer when she handed me a towel for my leg. I slowly cut the plastic ties while he was distracted. He left the phone on the coffee table in front of me, so I leaned forward from time to time to text "help" to your number when his back was turned. I was afraid he would catch me at any moment. Dee knew what I was doing and kept him distracted. She's the brave one."

The paramedics arrived and one started to tend to Porsche's leg and my arm.

ALL OF A SUDDEN, Tammy rose up. "Shhhitttt, I KNOW WHEN TO PLAY FUCKIN' DEAD. Y'all got some fucked up shit going on in here and you got me fucked up! You can't get this bitch that easy. I'm getting the hell outta here. If I don't see y'all muthafuckas another day in this life, it'll be too soon. Porsche, Bitch don't you call me no damn mo."

Tammy looked at the blood on the floor from Dee's body and turned to me. She said, "Xander, WHEN IT COMES DOWN TO IT; WE ALL GOT SHIT TO PAY FOR. TODAY HAPPENED TO BE YO DAY. SEE YO ASS IN HELL!"

And like that, Tammy got up and walked out. The detective told her not to leave. She yelled; "I know, I know. Don't leave town; y'all got questions. You know how to find me; y'all can't make me stay, I'm out!"

# 38

## Porsche

Marcus and I went to the hospital in separate ambulances. The police asked us countless questions. I assumed our stories lined up because we were both able to leave the hospital the next day. I had so many questions and I felt only Marcus could answer them. My heart ached that I lost the love of my life and the friend of my life. I wondered what would happen to Jay and whatever happened to Tye.

Marcus offered to help me find another place to live and gave me a lump sum of money to what he said, "start afresh." He made a couple of phone calls and later an older gentleman came by to introduce himself. He was a caramel-toned brother. He was built like a retired football player who stayed in shape. I laughed to myself because his suit was sort of tight. He never gave his name, but he said I would see his face from time to time. He gave me a cell phone and made it clear I should use it for life or death only. He said if I ever used it; I should throw it away immediately after the phone call. I looked at Marcus and he said; "Porsche, ask no questions and I'll tell you no lies." I got the point and took the phone. I took a deep breath and said, "New me, here I come."

# 39

# *Jay*

Once again, I'm in a dirty almond-colored cell, trapped like a hamster on a wheel. There's no way they got away again, NO WAY! I sat on the hard thin mattress with my head resting in my hands. I replayed my plan over and over. Play by play, moment by moment. I thought about all the time and energy I put into getting retribution. I thought about how I could have done something differently. I thought so long and hard. So much so, until I became angrier by the minute. I jumped up and laid on the floor and started doing sit-ups like my life depended on it. One...two...three...four...before I knew it I had done 100 sit-ups. I fell back on the cold filthy floor with my hands above my head. I stared at the rust-stained walls, water damaged ceiling and wondered how the hell I'm going to get out of this. I closed my eyes and thought about all the chances I passed to just kill that bitch at the office and walk away. I thought about how I could have ended Tammy the first night I met her. FUCK! They can't get away like this, not again.

All of a sudden, my train of thought was broken.

"Inmate. You've got a visitor, get dressed."

I opened my eyes and turned to see this little, short-ass jailer. He looked like he had seen a ghost. His voice trembled when he talked. He swallowed hard after he spoke as if he was trying to choke down all the nervousness he tried to hide. I stood up slowly, put on my button-down and tucked it in. *I knew this familiar routine.*

I stood at the door of the cell and put my hands out waiting on the cuffs. I could hear the cuffs jingling in the jailor's hands because he was so nervous. Although I found humor in that, I decided to give the dude a little advice. As soon as I heard the cuffs click, I said; "Yo my man. If you ever want to make it here, don't let 'em see weakness. That's what they look for. You coming to my cell shaking and shit. Put some bass in your voice man or else you going to be smuggling contraband for some crew or even worse, getting yo ass fucked up in here. Do you have family?

He looked like he didn't know if he should answer that or not. I said; "Well, do you?"

He nodded his head yes and said; "yeah man, a wife and kid."

I shook my head and said; "Man, don't answer that shit. You keep your personals, personal; you feel me? Strictly business in here lil man."

He looked at me like he understood and like he wanted to thank me for the tidbit of information but decided not to. We reached the visitation room. He removed the cuffs and said; "aight inmate, you got an hour."

I looked down at him and sucked my teeth. I could tell, he was taking heed to what I said because that quick, he tried to straighten up and have a little authority in his tone. I looked around the room and noticed a few women sitting there. Some crying, some fussing at some badass kids and others sitting with their arms folded, obviously mad for one reason or another. I glared around the room not having a clue who was here to see me. Suddenly, a hand waved my way and motioned for me to sit across from him.

He said, "So you just couldn't let it go, could you? Now look. All you had! All you had accomplished! Gone! And for what?"

Hurt and disappointed my efforts weren't appreciated, I reverted to that little 15-year-old boy. I sat there almost pouting. We sat in silence for seconds that seemed like hours.

Suddenly, he got up. He leaned towards me and said, "I'm going to do what I should have done a long time ago. I'm going to protect you. You keep your head low, and you'll be out of here soon. Trust me everyone will get what's owed. And I mean everyone!"

He stood up and motioned for me to stand. I was much taller, but at that point, I felt like I was reaching up to him. I felt this uneasiness in asking, but I said; "What do you plan to do?"

He walked a few steps towards the door and said, "like I said, protect you and fix this once and for all."

And like that Tye walked away. I stood up, put my shoulders back and with a sense of relief and pride, headed back to my cell. At that moment, I knew it would be okay.

LaTarsha Terry has always loved writing. At an early age she started writing poetry and discovered her love for writing. She progressed from writing poetry to short stories and utilized her writing as an outlet and found peace in doing so. LaTarsha was reluctant to share her stories, so she kept them to herself. She shared her talent as a writer in a college paper. Her professor noted she was a great writer; however she didn't use the correct writing style and deducted points. Although disappointed by the point deduction; LaTarsha found solace in knowing someone noticed her passion and recognized her talent. LaTarsha worked as a Certified Pharmacy Technician since 2001 and a Register Nurse

since 2007. Although she enjoys healthcare, she never lost the need and desire to write. She loves how the flow and rhythm of words come together to paint a picture that imprints on the mind of the reader. After the sudden loss of her father in 2020; LaTarsha decided to focus and pursue what gives her joy. She completed her first book in 2021 and looks forward to doing so much more.

# Coming Soon

When It Comes Down to It –

- Xander's Road to Marcus

- Tammy – They Made Me Do It

- Porsche – Lonely Lane to Love

- Tye's Redemption, Jay's Revenge

**Contact LaTarsha Terry @ whenitcomesdowntoitthebook.com**